Conveniently Yours

MELODY RAINNE

About the Author

Melody Rainne is a new romance author who lives in a small town in Michigan's Upper Peninsula. She is married to her husband of nine years and has two children.

Also by Melody Rainne

Tell Me You're Mine

How Winter Nights

Chapter One

Camden Luxmore.

One of the top CEOs in the country. And the youngest. He had recently risen to that position within the company and it had caused a lot of upset and resentment. Particularly from his brother, who had long coveted the position.

Desmond Luxmore, Camden's older brother, was no more qualified to be CEO than I was. But it was all he ever wanted. He didn't care to take the time to actually learn the business or how to run it. He figured since he was the oldest son that the position would just be handed to him and that there would be plenty of time to learn on the job. In his mind, it was his right.

It didn't matter to him that his younger brother spent every day since he was a teen following in their father's footsteps and learning everything he could about Luxmore Inc. He didn't care that while he partied every weekend on yachts with models that Camden studied independently and alongside their father. He still believed that no matter what he did, the company would be his solely on the fact that he was a Luxmore, and also the oldest.

Camden spent every single second of his free time studying and working, getting to know the ins and out of the business. He knew how to read people, how to worm his way into the hearts of investors and partners. Camden could achieve anything he set his mind to.

But he's a bit of an asshole. And also my boss.

I have worked as Camden's secretary for about eight years now. I know more about the man than I care to. I have watched him take Luxmore Inc from just barely getting by to being ranked number one globally. I have no idea how he did it, but he sure made it look easy.

Now that I think about it, it may be from the fact he gave up his entire childhood. Voluntarily. He actually enjoyed the business and all the challenges that came along with it. He loved problem solving, making deals, meetings, all the stuff that normal people hate.

He's tough, rarely giving anyone a second chance, but he gets the job done. I wouldn't say he's exactly feared by his employees, but it can get a little tense around here at times. Especially if he's in the building. Camden works a lot on the road, flying all over the country for meetings or to snag a new partnership, checking on all the branches personally to make sure they're running as smoothly as they should. Personally, I think he gets a kick out of scaring the shit out of his employees when they see him walk into the building for an unexpected visit.

Most days, there was no drama here at the company. Today though, is an entirely different story.

With one hand on the door to Camden's office, I freeze. My heart is beating wildly in my chest. It's my job to keep Mr Luxmore informed on everything that goes on in the company and tell him immediately of any problems that arise. I have been doing so for eight years now. But it never seems to get any easier. Especially when it involves a family member.

Delaying this certainly wouldn't help either.

I took a deep breath and knocked on the door before entering. The entire wall on the right side of his desk consisted of floor to ceiling windows. Camden was standing at the window looking out at the scenery. He was wearing his black work pants that hugged his tight ass perfectly and a white button-up shirt with the sleeves rolled up just past his elbows. His usual outfit. He looked perfect.

I'd be lying if I said I didn't sometimes enjoy the view. Both of them.

He may be my boss but I wasn't blind.

I cleared my throat. "Mr Luxemore, we have a situation."

I followed behind him and filled him in as we marched to Trent's office. Trent is the Executive Director of Luxmore Inc, as well as his Uncle. Everyone here respected him and thought he was a decent man. Someone to look up to.

Until today.

"Trent!" Camden growled as he threw open the doors to his office. His Uncle was startled, dropping the stack of papers he held in his hands.

"Camden," he said, placing his hand on his chest. "What can I do for you?" His eyes shifted nervously between me and Camden, searching for an answer.

Camden paced in front of Trent's desk, watching him grow more nervous by the second. I'm sure he was enjoying this. Finally, he stopped pacing, slamming both hands down on the desk. "Do you have any idea what you have done?" Camden asked, his voice eerily calm.

"I. . . I haven't done anything," he stammers,

looking to me for help. I quickly lowered my eyes to the floor and took a step back. I was staying out of this mess.

"That's bullshit and you know it," Camden answered, running his hand impatiently through his hair.

"You and I both know what you did. You put this company at risk with your reckless behavior."

Trent didn't even have the decency to look even the least bit ashamed. He stood a little straighter and cleared his throat. "You can't fire me," he states, staring at Camden with a smug look on his face. "I'm family."

"What the hell does that have to do with anything?" Camden replies. "This may be a family business, *our* family business, but that doesn't give you the right to do whatever and apparently whoever you want and just expect to be able to get away with it. We have rules here. We have standards. What you have done goes against everything that Luxmore Inc stands for. And I, for one, will not tolerate it."

The anger in Trent was so intense that his entire face was beet-red. I'm surprised you couldn't see smoke pouring out of his ears. "When your father hears . . ."

Camden cut him off, having no more patience for the man. "It doesn't matter what my father hears, he stepped down ages ago." He took a few steps towards

Trent, who backed up until his legs hit the side of his desk. Trent put a hand down on the desk to steady himself. Camden towered over his uncle, and he bent his head down to look him in the eyes. "I am the boss now. That's something you seem to have forgotten. And I will not tolerate this kind of behavior or your bullshit any longer. I certainly will not tolerate your threats. A grown ass man," he scoffed, "threatening to tell my daddy on me. You're pathetic," he spat.

"Please," Trent pleaded, falling to his knees. "Give me one more chance. I'll do anything. I know I fucked up but I can't lose my job." It was the exact opposite of how he acted just a minute ago. A man that acted in this manner was dangerous. He couldn't be trusted. I know for a fact that he didn't really give a shit about this job or the company. All he really cared about was his status. He feared nothing more than becoming an outsider. Especially an outsider of one of the most powerful and influential families.

He knew that once you were cast out, there was no going back.

"There's nothing more we can do for you," Camden waved away his begging. "Actually, there's nothing I *want* to do for you."

"I've been here for thirty years," Trent argued, as if that fact would make a difference to Camden.

He nods. "You have," Camden agreed. "But that doesn't excuse what you have done. You have done a lot for this company in your time here, and you may be my uncle, but what you have done goes against everything this company stands for. And I cannot turn a blind eye to that."

Trent hung his head, looking defeated. "Can you at least help bury the press that'll surely come of this?" he asked in a small voice.

"That, unfortunately, is too late," Camden stated, starting to sound bored with the whole situation. He never was one to linger over anything. "The reports that the now-former Executive Director of Luxmore Inc has been caught cheating on his wife, buying escorts, gambling, and stealing from investors has already hit newsstands and is all over the internet. You're on your own with this one. Now," he turned back to face his disgraced uncle, "Get out. You're fired." All the color drained from Trent's face. He really had thought that he was going to get away with all this. This just goes to show that having all the money in the world isn't a free pass for you to be an asshole.

Without listening to another word, Camden turned on his heels and walked out of the office, with me following close behind. We walked past the security guards and police sent in to collect all of his belongings and escort him to the police station and out of Luxemore Inc forever. All of his clearances, allowances, and privileges have already been disabled and revoked. He would no longer be allowed to freely walk inside Luxemore Inc, or any of its offices worldwide.

I followed Camden into his office and made him some tea. Alcohol wasn't allowed on the job so tea would have to do for now. Camden scrubbed his hand over his face as I set the teapot and mug in front of him. I could tell this was not how he wanted to start the day. We had been collecting data and evidence against Trent for months now, so we knew this day was coming. But it still didn't make it any easier.

Chapter Two

"Hey, Anna. What was all that?" Lisa asked as I sat down at my desk. Terry and John, our other two coworkers in this section, poked their heads around the corner, smelling gossip. I filled them all in, surprised that they didn't already know. Although, I guess there weren't that many people who would know. There were only a few people working behind the scenes to dig up the dirt on Trent. They didn't want rumors flying until it was confirmed and they certainly didn't want him tipped off that he was being looked into.

Lisa leaned back in her chair and whistled. "Yikes. What a way to start the day, huh?" she said, looking over at Terry and John, who both nodded in agreement. "What did he say to Trent? Does he look all sexy when he's angry, or does he get like, that giant vein in his forehead?" she asked, grabbing the arm of my chair and pulling me right next to her. I really hated these chairs on wheels. She looked over at Camden's office door, a sort of dreamy look in her eyes. "I always imagined he'd be sexy as hell when he's all angry and worked up," she sighed.

"Lisa!" I gasped, looking back at Camden's office door, which thankfully, remained closed. I would die of embarrassment if he happened to walk out and hear our conversation. "That's our boss you're talking about."

She looked back at me, shrugging her shoulders like it was no big deal. "I know. But it doesn't mean I can't appreciate the view of a good-looking man."

I had to agree with her there. Camden was perfect, visually speaking. Not that I would ever let anyone know that I thought that.

"I'm straight and even I agree with her," John pointed out.

"Will you two stop?" I scolded, looking between the two of them. He could walk out of his office any second now. My cheeks flamed. I love my coworkers but they are going to get me in trouble one of these days, I just know it.

"But seriously, Lisa, you find angry forehead veins sexy?"

She shrugged, "What can I say? I have unique tastes," she laughed.

"That's one way to put it," Terry teased her, shaking his head.

"What? Like you're so perfect?" Lisa asked him, folding her arms over her chest.

"You know it," Terry said before turning back to his computer to continue his work. John sat back at his own computer while Lisa scooted closer to me again.

"So what's he really like?" She whispered in my ear. I guess gossip time wasn't over with.

I sighed loudly, playing dumb. "What is who like?"

"Seriously?" She rolled her eyes at me. "Mr Luxmore. Camden. What's he like?"

"You've been here almost as long as I have, you know what his grumpy ass is like."

She shook her head. "That's not what I mean. I know what 'boss-man' Camden is like. What is 'real-man' Camden like?"

I look over at her, eyebrows raised in amusement. "Real-man Camden? What is that supposed to mean?"

"You know," she says, lowering her voice and looking around to make sure no one was listening. "What's he like when he's not working? Who is the great Camden Luxmore when he's at home?"

"How should I know?"

"You're with him everyday. The two of you go everywhere together."

"It's alway work related," I pointed out. "And nothing more."

"Still," Lisa rolled her eyes again. "You're the only woman he lets around him. In fact, you're the only woman I have ever seen him with since I started working here," she said, her eyebrows raised in accusation. She better not be trying to say what I think she is. "He has women chasing after him everywhere he goes, but he only seems to have eyes for you."

My cheeks are on fire. "That's not true."

"Oh, yes it is," Terry chimed in, coming around the corner. How long had he been there? How long had he been listening? "Like Lisa, I haven't seen any other woman get close to him besides you. Haven't you ever heard the rumors?"

My chest tightened. "Rumors?"

"Crap. I guess you didn't know. They kind of died down long ago, but there was once rumors floating around that you and the boss were . . ." he wiggled his eyebrows.

"Doing it in his office," Lisa finished for him. Terry nodded in agreement.

"What the hell? Seriously?" I asked in a loud whisper. My eyes flicked to Camden's office door, still closed. People really thought that about me? And him? I've never thought about Camden that way. He was my boss, and that was it. Thinking back, I've never done anything that would have given anyone reason to think that I was doing the boss.

Right?

"Oh, don't worry, sweetie. Like I said, they died down years ago," Terry assured me.

"What gave people that idea in the first place?" I asked.

"He's a good looking man. Everywhere he goes he has tons of women throwing themselves at him, but he never acknowledges their existence. Doesn't even say one word to them. I don't think he's ever had a girl-friend. But you, on the other hand," they both look at me. I suddenly feel like I'm getting scolded in the prin-cipal's office. "You walk side by side with him at these events. He talks to you, gets in all close and whispers in your ear. You ride together in the same car. People see. People talk. People get jealous."

"I go with him to these events because they are work events. I walk beside him because I'm his secre-tary. And he talks to me and whispers things to me because one, there's something work related he needs to tell me and two, it often gets loud at those things. And you know he doesn't drive, so he calls me to do that for him. That's all there is to it." I say, a little angry that I have to even have to say these things out loud. I shouldn't have to explain things and defend myself when all I was doing was my job.

Terry grabbed my arm lightly and patted it. "Let it go, girl. No one talks about it anymore. No one thinks you're banging the boss. I'm sorry I brought it up."

Now that he did though I doubt I'd ever be able to get it off my mind. Camden was a sexy man, anyone could see that. Have I ever thought about what it would be like to have him touch me all over? Or kiss me with his full lips of his?

No, I have not.

But I sure was now. My thighs involuntarily clenched at these new unwanted thoughts. I had to excuse myself to the bathroom to calm myself down. I should not be having these kinds of thoughts at work. Or at all. It was extremely inappropriate and unprofessional of me.

He was confident. Sure, he was a little cocky at times, but weirdly, it was also a little sexy. Camden Luxmore was a man who knew what he wanted, and he went after it. He never settled for anything less than he wanted, anything less than what he felt he deserved.

Camden and I had a working relationship. That was it. Nothing more, nothing less. Sure, I was with him all the time, sometimes day and night, and most weekends. It didn't leave any time to look for a real relationship, but that fact didn't really bother me. I wasn't looking for one anyway, it would just distract me from work, and I love my job. I don't mind all the extra hours and tasks put on me. I love it. I welcome new challenges. This is what I've always wanted to do.

I ran my fingers through my hair and fixed my makeup before returning to my desk, getting knowing looks from all three of my coworkers as I passed by each one of them.

"Ms Collins, may I see you in my office for a minute?" Camden poked his head out of his office.

Shit. "Um, yea, I'll be right there," I answered. I felt the heat creep up the back of my neck. How much had he heard? I gave my coworkers a look that said I would deal with them later. Terry made a kissy face at me, and I quickly flipped him off before standing up and straightening my skirt and blouse. This was the first time I was in trouble with the boss.

It made me nervous as hell.

Chapter Three

"You have a call," Camden informed me the second I entered his office. He nodded towards the phone on his desk. "It's your sister apparently." He turned back towards me, with a look of anger in his eyes. "You know how I feel about personal phone calls at work."

"Uh, I . . ."

"Should answer it," he interrupted.

"I . . . yes. Sorry," I stammered before hurrying over to his desk. No one ever calls for anyone but Camden on that phone. It was his line, and his alone.

I picked up the receiver, my hands shaking. "Hello?" I said. I could feel Camden's eyes on me, making me even more nervous. I turned my back to him to try to get at least a little privacy. I wasn't about to ask my boss to leave his own office. I was in enough trouble as it is.

"Where have you been?!" My sister's voice screamed into my ear. I actually had to pull the phone away from my ear, she was so loud.

"I've been at work, where do you think?"

She sounded out of breath. "Your house caught fire! It's gone, I'm so sorry. I've been trying to get a hold of you all morning. I left about a million messages on your cell"

My heart dropped. "What?" I asked, dropping the phone. Camden, seeing the shock across my face, picked it up and asked Julia what's going on.

I couldn't believe it. My brain did not want to process Julia's words.

"Come on," Camden said, grabbing me by my wrist and pulling me out of the office. I went with him, ignoring the concerned looks and questions from my coworkers. I was in no state to answer any of their questions right now. I didn't even know the exact details of the situation myself.

Before I knew it we were at my house. Well, what was left of my house. We pulled up to a mess of debris, smoke, ashes, and people all over the street gawking and wondering what was going on.

It was true. My house was gone, everything was

gone. Everything I owned, every sentimental thing, every memory I had, gone.

Forever.

I spotted my sister and ran into her arms, crying. "I'm so sorry, sis," she said, stroking my hair. "I tried to get a hold of you."

"It wouldn't have made a difference if you had," I shook my head. "How did this happen?"

Julia shrugged. "Your guess is as good as mine, babe. They're still trying to figure it out."

"Well, I'm glad you're here," I told her, meaning it.

"Me too." She hugged me tighter. "But what's he doing here?" She whispered, nodding towards Camden, who was over talking with the police and firemen. He had a very serious look on his face. It made me nervous all over again.

"He . . ." I don't know why he was here, honestly. And *how* did we get here? Camden didn't drive. I know this because I'm the one who drove him anywhere. I didn't even know if he had his license or not to tell you the truth.

Camden finished with the police and walked over to us. Julia released her hold on me. "They can't tell the immediate cause of the fire. That's going to take some time to investigate. And they also don't think that there's anything salvageable," he informed us.

I took in a shaky breath. What the hell am I supposed to do? "Seriously? Nothing?"

He shook his head.

I stared at the pile of rubble that used to be my home, my life.

What do I do now?

Julia's phone pinged with a text. "Shit," she grumbled. "Two of my kids have the flu and Mark's getting overwhelmed watching them by himself."

"I got her," Camden told her. "You go take care of your family."

"Are you sure?" She asked, as shocked as I was. Camden never seemed to care about anyone but himself. This was a widely known fact about him.

"Absolutely. Go."

Julia hugged me once more. "You sure you're going to be okay?" she whispered. I nodded, even though it was a lie.

She looked at Camden, not sure what to believe. But when her phone went off she mouthed the words *call me* before running to her car to go take care of her sick kids.

"Come on," Camden said, leading me to his car.

I stopped in my tracks. "Come where? I have no place to go," I said, the realization finally sinking in. My house has been reduced to a pile of ash and the only family I had left was Julia, but she was married and had four kids. Even if two of them weren't suffering from the flu there was no way I'd want to stay there. No room, no privacy. I imagine it would be super loud and crazy all the time.

I'm homeless.

"To my house," he answered. "You need a place to stay, and I've got the room. It shouldn't be too awkward since you've been there a lot already, right?"

That was true, I do pick him up for work and drop him off there a lot. And I occasionally do come over to help with some work related business if he happens to be working late and bring it home with him instead of staying in the office. But to stay in my boss's house? I don't know about that.

"I, uh . . ."

"Need a place to stay," he finished for me. "And I have more than enough room. Let's go," he said, holding open the car door for me.

Not seeing any other option, I got in the car.

Chapter Four

Walking into Camden's house felt different this time. I've been here almost every day either to pick him up, drop him off, or some other kind of work thing, and I never thought anything of it. But today just feels different.

Camden cleared his throat. "Feel free to make yourself at home," he said, looking around awkwardly. Checking his watch, he added, "I've got to get back to the office. I have back to back meetings in a bit."

"Oh, I'll come with you then." I've never missed a meeting before and I don't intend to start now.

"No," he said, putting up a hand to stop me. "You just lost your house and everything you own. You're taking the rest of the day off. And tomorrow if you need. This is not a suggestion."

I opened my mouth to argue, but shut it again. As much as I hated to admit it, I knew he was right. I wouldn't be able to concentrate much at work and I really wouldn't be of any help if I was there.

Camden nods once, taking my silence as me agreeing. "I'll be back tonight, make yourself at home," he says before turning to leave.

"Wait! Should I at least drive you?" I've been doing it for him for so long that it would feel strange not to, even with my circumstance.

He shakes his head. "I can drive myself. You stay here and rest."

Come to think of it, he did drive me to my house and then here. "How long exactly have you been able to drive, and if so, why have I been the one doing it almost every day?"

Camden looked at me with a crooked smile on his face and shrugged. "I've always been able to. I just prefer it when you do."

Jerk. Does he know how much more sleep I could have gotten if I didn't have to wake up early and also stay late to play chauffeur to him? Then again, would he really care? He's Camden Luxmore, in love with himself and no one else.

After he left for work I didn't know what to do

with myself so I went and took a seat on the couch in the sunken living room. Besides the backyard with the man made pond and water fountains, this was my favorite place in his house. It was practical yet comfortable. Styled like the rest of the house in black and silver colors, it was exactly how you'd think Camden Luxmore would live.

Not that I often think about what he's like at home.

My eyes wandered over to his bedroom door. What *was* Camden like when he wasn't in the office, scaring the life out of his employees and making deals with foreign investors? It's not like he runs around the office terrorizing everyone that works there or anything like that. Camden just didn't tolerate nonsense at work. Or in any aspect of his life, really. We were there to get the job done and he expected us all to be on an extremely professional level, at all times.

There were no second chances with him, either. If you didn't fit into his standard or if you messed up, he wouldn't hesitate to reprimand and shame you. Again, not that it was something he did on purpose, the man just saw the world differently I suppose. The rich and powerful were a different breed after all.

I can't imagine him not working at all, even for one

second. I don't think, in all the years I've worked for him, that I've seen him relax at all. The man was always busy, always coming up with a new idea or product, always on the phone with someone trying to make a deal, always negotiating something. I'm not sure he even knew how to relax.

I don't think I'll be able to right now, either. Not when everything in my life just literally went up in smoke. Yes, it's all materialistic stuff, but it was mine. It was everything I had worked for. It was things from my childhood and things that were my parents', and all the memories that came with them.

I think that's what I was most sad to lose, the memories. I'd catch a glimpse of an old stuffed animal or toy, or be looking through an old photo album and immediately be brought back to when I was little and playing with it, or to the vacations we would always take together as a family.

Those were the kind of memories I would cherish forever.

They were also the kind of memories we could never make again. Both of our parents were gone, lost to a car accident years ago.

It's just me and Julia now.

I try not to think of that day anymore. The day

when my family was ripped apart. The day that everything changed.

I shake my head to bring myself back to the present. There was no need to fall back down that dark hole again. Not when I have something else to worry about in the present.

I want to explore the rest of the house but I don't feel comfortable enough to just wander around without Camden's permission. Yes, he told me to make myself at home, but does anyone really do that at someone else's house? It just doesn't feel right.

I finally decided to just go take a bath in my room. Attached to the guest room I was staying in was a huge bathroom with a massive tub in it. It was big enough that I could lay in it and submerge my entire body.

I lit some candles I had found stashed in a drawer, filling the air with the relaxing scent of lavender. Next I poured in some bubble bath and set the water to hot. I needed the heat to melt away my tense muscles and the stress of the day.

I slipped into the water, sinking all the way down so just my head was above water. It felt magical. I could immediately feel some of the stress leaving my body. I breathed in the steam, trying to forget about the eventful morning we just had. So much had happened within such a short time. I allowed my tears to fall, mingling with the bathwater. No one was here to see them. No one was here to see and share my pain. I let it all out, everything that I was feeling. I tried so hard to keep it all together, but there was only so much that I could take. I cried until there was nothing left.

Taking a deep breath, I leaned back against the cool side of the tub and closed my eyes. I was determined not to let everything get to me too much. I had to stay strong. I wasn't the type of woman who would just fall apart. I had to stay sharp, to stay focused. Tomorrow I had to go back to work and do my job. I couldn't take any more time off. My sister needed me. Sure, she had her own job, but she had a large family to take care of. And I had to make sure that I was always in a position to help her. She never once asked for it but since our parents died I felt responsible for her. She was all I had left in this world.

I sank down in the tub, letting the hot water wash all my worries away. I needed a clear mind if I was going to be able to deal with everything tomorrow. As I lay soaking my mind drifted off to thoughts of Camden. Besides passing out on his couch after working extra hours here on projects, I've never actually stayed the night at his house.

He would be sleeping in the room right next to me.

Just the thought of that had me feeling and thinking all kinds of inappropriate things. My hands made their way down between my legs, my fingers skimming just over my opening. I let my mind wander, imagining what it would feel like to have Camden touch me all over, having his hands and lips on every inch of body. I imagined the look in his eyes as he hovered over me, and my body quivered in need. I arched my back, as he lowered his body, positioning himself right at my entrance.

"Having a nice bath?" Camden's voice broke through my thoughts.

My eyes flew open, finding my boss standing over me. I quickly scrambled to cover my body, even though I'm more than sure he already got an eye full. My cheeks flamed from embarrassment. How long had he been standing there?

Camden looked away but couldn't hide the smirk on his face, confirming my fear. He cleared his throat. "I um, I bought you some new clothes and things," he said, looking a little uncomfortable.

"You did?"

He nodded. "While we were at your house this morning I noticed all your clothes and other belongings had all caught fire. I figured you'd need new things. I set everything on the bed in your room," he gestured with a nod.

I've never seen this side of him before. Camden was actually being kind and sweet. "Thank you," I whispered. His kindness had tears pricking at the back of my eyes. I already promised myself I wouldn't cry over what happened today. And I really didn't want to cry in front of my boss.

Especially when I was still naked and in the tub.

I cleared my throat and he took that as his cue to leave.

"Yes, well, I guessed at your size as far as the clothes go and I picked things I thought were your taste. If there's anything that doesn't work we'll take it back and exchange it," he said without looking at me. "I'm going to start dinner so come on out whenever you're ready," he added before finally leaving the room.

I let out the breath I was holding in and sunk back down in the water. There was so much to process right now. First, how much did Camden actually see? The bubbles I had at the start of my bath were pretty much non-existent now, offering him way more of a view than I'd like him to see.

The fact that he went out and replaced a lot of the items I lost in my house fire made my heart swell. He really didn't have to do any of this. Just letting me stay here for a while was more than enough for me.

I climbed out the tub, throwing on my robe. Walking into my temporary bedroom I was greeted to the sight of more shopping bags than I'd ever seen in one place before. He must have spent a fortune on all of this.

There were clothes for every occasion and season, ranging from cold weather to hot, pajamas to casual to black tie affairs.

There was jewelry and makeup, hairbrushes and skincare. Anything I could possibly need and more was here in this room.

His kindness overwhelmed me. It was one thing to take me into his home, giving me a place to sleep. It was an entirely different thing to run out and make sure every one of my needs was met. I swiped at the tears that fell down my face. No one had ever done anything like this for me. I had spent the last few years making sure everyone else was taken care of. This was new for me, and I'm not sure if I'd ever be able to get used to it.

After a quick search through most of my new clothes I decided on an outfit that was both comfortable and casual. It felt strange to wear anything but formal or work clothes in front of Camden. This whole experience was going to take some time to get used to.

I walk out to find Camden in the kitchen, just like he promised. I honestly had no idea the man could cook. Usually he either ordered something from one of the fancy restaurants around here or I whipped up something quick for him. I wasn't the best cook, but it seemed to be good enough for him. He never once complained.

"You look good," he says when he sees me, eyeing me up and down. He nods once as if approving his shopping choice. I have to admit, he did know how to pick out clothes. It made me wonder how many other women he did this for.

A hint of jealousy twisted in my gut. Camden with other women is not something I have ever really thought about before. He always seemed too busy to date, like I was, so I just never pictured it before.

I didn't like it.

"Thank you," I said, looking down to try to hide the blush that lit my face on fire.

He smiled briefly, before turning his attention back to the vegetables that needed to be chopped. He was still wearing his work clothes, and had his sleeves rolled up just past his elbows. I couldn't help but stare as he washed all the vegetables at the sink.

I wondered what he would do if I just walked up right behind him, wrapping my arms around his waist. Holding him tight, while pressing my cheek into his back. What would it feel like to have him turn me around, holding me in those muscular arms of his? My heart raced thinking about him staring into my eyes, as he lowered his lips to mine . . .

I try my best to avoid more thoughts like this as he finishes up with the cooking. I make myself useful by setting the table. It also helped to serve as a distraction. Until he came to set all the food on the table. Camden leaned over me to set the salad bowl down. He was so close that I could feel the heat coming off his skin.

Both my mind and my heart went haywire.

Dinner was quiet, but nice. After we had both finished I offered to help with the dishes but he refused, telling me I should go and relax instead.

After my shower I put on a new pair of pajamas and climbed into bed. Just as I was reaching to turn off the bedside lamp a text from Julia came. I let her know that I was okay, and assured her that no, Camden didn't have anything in mind other than to help me. I know she was just being overprotective. She was wary of other men, especially when it had to do with her little sister. I appreciated it, but at the same time wished she would just let me make my own decisions about people. I have known Camden for years. We have worked closely together and I pretty much knew all there was to know about the man. I trusted him with my life.

I laid down and closed my eyes, even though I knew sleep wouldn't be coming easy tonight. My thoughts and emotions were causing a storm inside my head.

Chapter Five

I was woken up the next morning by the sound of someone rummaging around in my room. They were gone before I could fully drag myself out of bed. I got up to find a complete set of clothes set out for me. I guess that's what I would be wearing for the day. I took the stack of neatly folded clothes to the bathroom to get dressed, in case whoever it was decided to come back to my room for whatever reason. No one wants a stranger to see them naked.

I walk out to the kitchen to find Camden already seated at the table, drinking his coffee and looking over some papers for work.

Seriously, didn't the man ever take a break?

Sitting down, I cleared my throat. "Um, Mr

Luxmore, who was that in my room this morning?" I was really hoping it wasn't him snooping around. But then again, having a stranger in there wasn't much better.

He looked at me with a confused look on his face for a second before answering. "Oh, that must have been Gretta. She's your own personal maid that I hired. She'll attend to your every need and make sure everything is taken care of for you."

A personal maid? For me? I shifted uncomfortably in my seat. I've never had a maid before and I wasn't too sure I liked the idea of having one. I've always done everything myself and I was more than capable of continuing to do so. This was only a temporary arrangement anyway, until I could find a new place to live. There was no need for someone to take care of me like this.

"Thank you, but I don't need a maid," I whispered.

Camden tilted his head and looked at me. "Are you sure? I hired her specifically to make things easier for you."

I suddenly felt bad. He was just trying to do something nice for me. Was I being ungrateful? Should I just let another grown woman wash and fold all my clothes, setting out outfits for my day each morning?

Should I let her clean up after me so I don't have to lift a finger? I shook my head. It didn't feel right to me.

"I'm sorry. I do appreciate everything you're doing for me, really. I just prefer to do things for myself."

Camden looked lost in thought for a minute before finally nodding his head. "Alright. If that's what you want."

I let out a sigh of relief. "Thank you."

"Gretta," he called. "Can you come here for a second?" She seemed to appear out of nowhere, stopping before Camden and staring at the floor. Was she not allowed to look him in the eye? Were any of his staff? "Gretta, there's been a change in plans. Your services are no longer needed."

I looked over at him in horror as Gretta simply nodded and began to walk away, accepting her fate.

"Wait!' I all but yelled. Gretta stopped in her tracks. "You're firing her?" I asked Camden.

"Well, yes, You said you don't need a maid. I hired her specifically for you. What else would you have me do?"

I looked at the poor woman. I'm sure she could get a job somewhere else, but I felt awful that I got her fired on her first day. And she hadn't done a single thing wrong. "You can't just fire her," I argued.

Camden crossed his arms over his chest. "First, you

say you don't need her, now you don't want me to fire her. Which is it?"

"I . . ." I didn't know what to do. I closed my mouth and looked down at my breakfast, getting cold on the table in front of me.

Camden sighed heavily. "How about this - Gretta, we no longer need you. But," he turned to look at me while still speaking to her, "I will still give you a full year's pay." He raised an eyebrow at me as if to say 'See, I'm not a total ass.'

Gretta finally lifted her gaze to Camden. "You mean it?" She asked, tears in her eyes.

"I do," he nodded simply. "In fact, I'll have it ready for you by the end of the day." Tears flowed down her face as she thanked him over and over. It had me nearly in tears as well.

I looked over at the man sitting across the table from me and smiled. Camden Luxmore just may have a heart after all.

We drove to work as usual, but like everything else, it felt different this time. I had just spent the night at our boss's house, and it wasn't for a work related reason. Everyone was going to find out. I just know they were.

My heart began to pound. What would they even

think? I stole a look at Camden in the mirror. He was reading over something on his iPad. He didn't seem like any of this affected him. And why should it? It's not like anything happened between us.

Or was ever going to.

But oh, if only they could read my mind . . .

We arrive at work and I'm immediately swarmed by my coworkers. They must have heard the news of what happened to my house. I looked to Camden for help but he was already gone, as if both me and my problems no longer existed to him.

What did I expect, really?

"Oh my god, are you okay?" Lisa asked, eyes wide with worry.

Josh came up to me, put his hands on my shoulders, slowly turning me around to check for any injuries. "You didn't get hurt, did you?"

Terry just walked over, throwing his arms around me. "We were so worried about you," he cried.

See, this is why I love these guys. "I'm fine," I answered, hugging them all back. "I promise, I am okay. My house on the other hand . . ."

Terry let out a little whimper. "It's ok," I assured him. "It's just a house," I say, trying to sound more confident than I really was. Inside I was a complete mess. A shaking, crying, confused mess. But there was no way that I would ever show anyone that side of me. Especially Camden. I couldn't look weak in front of any of them.

Looking at the pity and sadness on their faces has me wondering if I had made a mistake in coming to work today. Maybe I should have stayed at Camden's house for one more day. Hidden in the safety of the big fluffy comforters on my bed. Well, Camden's bed. I shake away the naughty thoughts that were beginning to creep into my head. Now was not the time to be thinking about my boss in bed.

Was there ever a good time to think about your boss in bed?

"How do you feel?" Lisa asked as we walked to our desk. Lisa and I shared a long desk together right outside of Camden's office. She also had her own private one near John and Terry. It was more efficient for him to have two of us here. "What can I get you?" She continued. "Do you need anything? I may have some spare furniture or something in my storage unit. I'll admit I haven't been in there for a while and I'm not entirely sure of its current condition, but I bet I could find you something useful," she offered.

My heart warmed at my friend's generosity. And

also John and Terry, with how much they seemed to care. They were all so concerned about me. In a weird way, it made me feel really good. It was comforting knowing that I always had someone to watch my back. I tend to forget about it a lot, with having to take care of my sister and worry about her. I've always put everyone else before myself. I was never one to put my needs first. It felt selfish, especially when other people depended on me.

"I'm okay," I shake my head. "I promise. I'm actually staying . . . with a friend right now," I lie. There was no way in hell anyone was going to find out the truth about where I was staying. Could you imagine the rumors? How would I be able to face anyone at work after that?

"Oh, good," Lisa let out a breath, visibly relieved. "That's one less thing you have to worry about then. But seriously," she said, turning towards me and gripping my arm with both hands, "if you need anything at all, please don't hesitate to ask."

"Same with us!" Terry called from the other side of the wall. I smiled at their blatant eavesdropping. I really loved these guys.

The rest of the workday went by pretty much uneventfully. Word had gotten out about what had happened and people would occasionally stop by and ask how I was and if I needed anything.

That evening Camden insisted on driving home together. It felt strange, almost wrong to be seated in the passenger side. I usually do all the driving for him.

I walk out into the living room after changing out of my work clothes to find Camden sitting on the couch. "Should I make us something for dinner?" I offer. He cooked last time so I thought it was only fair that I do it this time.

Camden held up the stack of papers I didn't see in his hands. "I have a ton of work to catch up on. I won't have time to eat for a few hours. You can go ahead and make something for yourself if you'd like," he said without even stopping to look up at me. "I'll even get out of your way. I'll be in my home office," he added, gathering all of his work off the coffee table. I felt bad at kicking him out of his own space.

I took a seat where he had just been sitting on the couch. I was starving but wasn't really in the mood to cook. I wasn't comfortable just rummaging around someone else's kitchen and fridge. Especially if they weren't going to be eating with me. I finally decided to just order a pizza and salad. Maybe I could get Camden to eat a quick bite. It wouldn't be good for him to skip any meals.

I waited a little over an hour to order dinner. Camden did look busy, so I wanted to make sure he had a little time to get some work done before I began bothering him with food. Once it arrived I put a couple slices on a plate along with a small bowl of salad. I walked over to his office door and, using my elbow, knocked softly.

"Yeah?" he calls, sounding a little weary.

I pushed open the door and held up the food. "Thought you could use this."

He sighed, standing up. "I guess I could use the break," he agreed. He took the dishes from me and headed back out to the living room. I grabbed some food for myself and joined him.

I couldn't help but sneak a few glances at him as we ate in silence. His hair was all messed up from repeatedly running his hands through it, and his shirt was unbuttoned a little, giving me a peak of his muscular chest. Camden had always been in work mode. Seeing him like this felt . . . almost intimate. I blush at the thought.

After we had finished eating, I cleared away the dishes and took care of the garbage and leftovers, while Camden went and picked out a bottle of wine for us to share. After finishing one glass he leaned back against the couch and closed his eyes. Within seconds he was snoring softly beside me. I quietly cleared away our glasses and found a blanket to place over him.

I took one last look at Camden, who now seemed more of a man to me than my boss, and flicked off the lights, heading to bed myself.

Chapter Six

"So how are you? How are things at home?" I ask Julia as we sit down at our favorite restaurant. We used to meet here several times a week before her kids got older and more involved in after school activities, sports, and clubs. Now we only get together once or twice a month at most.

Julia laughed. "I should be the one to ask you that."

"I'm fine," I waved her worry away.

"Are you though?" She asked again, taking a sip of her coffee. "God, I really needed that."

"Kids a handful?" I asked, holding back a laugh. I imagine raising four kids can't be easy. Hell, I can't imagine that even raising one is easy.

Julia sat back in the booth, staring off into the

corner. "I love them. I really do," she sighs, "but it is so tough sometimes. Have you ever tried to take care of four sick young people while at the same time being sick yourself?" Her eyes slid to me, giving me a look that says she already knows the answer.

I shook my head. I can honestly say I have not. "That sounds awful." I don't know how she does it.

"It is," she said, sighing heavily this time. "The twins brought the flu home from school and it quickly spread to their brothers, and then to me. This happens every year and I should be prepared for it. I don't know why it seems to surprise me every time. Mark was the only one who escaped the sickness. I sent him to his parents house while we all recovered."

Yikes. "That sounds awful. Couldn't you have used his help?"

Julia shrugged, "You know how he is when he's sick. I would have had to take care of *five* sick children while sick myself if he had stayed," she huffed out a laugh. I suppose that's true. Julia's husband did exaggerate any illness that he came down with. He caught the dreaded man-flu more times than I could count. He was an amazing father to his kids and the perfect husband to my sister, don't get me wrong. The man just could not handle being sick. "But everyone is all better now. Not so much as a sniffle in my household at the moment," she said proudly.

"Well, that's good news."

Julia nodded in agreement. "That it is. In fact, this is the first time I've been out of the house in weeks." She leaned back again and sighed. "This is almost like a mini vacation."

I laughed. Only Julia would consider sitting in a booth at a restaurant to be like a vacation.

"But seriously," she said, straightening up in her seat. She crossed her arms over her chest and looked at me, concern filling her eyes. "How are you doing?"

I shrugged. "I'm fine. Really."

"You've been staying at your boss's house now for a few weeks. Isn't he sick of you yet?"

I narrowed my eyes at her.

Sick of me? Rude.

"I don't think so," I answered honestly. He hasn't said anything to me at least that would indicate he wanted me gone. Hell, he would have just come right out and say it if he did. Camden isn't one to beat around the bush. He'll tell you exactly what's on his mind, whether you want to hear it or not. Or if it could hurt you or not. It's very rare for that man to care about the feelings of others. Not that he's a monster.

But still.

Julia just eyed me. "I still think you should come stay with me."

"And all of your kids?" I laughed. "Where would I even sleep?" I had been to their place many times. There's barely enough room for just the six of them. There was absolutely no way they could even fit a fraction of my stuff. And I would feel completely awful taking away any space for their children. I appreciated the thought though.

"Well, we have a couch," she laughed awkwardly.

"Yes, that would be wonderful for my back."

Julia eyed me again. I wish I could read her expression. "Is it really because of the excuses you just gave me or is it something else?"

"That's it. Promise," I answered honestly.

"Uh huh." She tilted her head, looking at me as though I wasn't being entirely truthful with her.

What was there for me to lie about?

"I think that you don't want to come stay with me, darling sister, because you like him."

"Like him?" My heart began to hammer in my chest at that thought. "You mean Camden? Camden Luxmore, my boss?" I scoffed. "No. No, there's absolutely no way. Don't be ridiculous."

Julia leaned back, a satisfied look spreading across

her face. "I knew it," she said smugly. "You totally love him."

Heat rushed to my face, and every other part of my body. I don't love him, I don't. He's my boss. We spend pretty much every day and night together, but it's for work purposes. Nothing more. He's comfortable, he's familiar, he's . . . holy crap. I think I might like my boss.

Chapter Seven

The first half of work flew by in a blur. I couldn't concentrate on anything work related. My mind kept drifting back to mine and Julia's conversation at the restaurant. And to Camden. There was absolutely no way I was into him.

"Are you ready for lunch?" Lisa asked, interrupting my thoughts. Right on cue, my stomach growled. "I guess you are," she said with a laugh.

I turned off my computer and grabbed Terry and John to join us. For as long as the four of us have worked together, we've always had lunch together. Because of the nature of my job, I didn't have too many friends. I was constantly busy with work. So these three were as close to best friends as I had.

We all sat down with our chicken wraps, salads,

and green smoothies. The four of us decided we all wanted to eat healthier a few weeks ago. Sitting at a computer all day, I have gotten into some pretty unhealthy snacking habits. And it was beginning to show.

"The salad is actually pretty tasty today," Terry commented. I nodded in agreement. Every ingredient did look a lot fresher than normal today. Not to say that we're ever served old, gross food here. Luxmore Inc takes really good care of its employees. Nothing but the best for us. It's one of the reasons I feel incredibly lucky to be able to work here.

All through lunch I noticed that John kept glancing at something to the left of him. I thought nothing of it at first, but then after like, the tenth time he looked my curiosity got the best of me.

"Hey John," I said, waving my hand a little to try and get his attention. He was now staring intensely at something across the cafeteria. "John!" I said again a little louder, kicking his foot under the table.

"Ouch," he replied dramatically, bending down to rub his foot. "What was that for?"

"Don't be so dramatic," I rolled my eyes. "I barely touched you."

"Still . . ."

"What do you keep staring at?" I asked.

John looked around before shushing me. "Keep it down, will you?"

"Sorry," I said, lowering my voice. I swear, this man was always so damn dramatic.

He set his fork down, leaning in closer like he was about to tell me some huge secret. "I think that table over there," he nodded slightly to his left, "keeps looking over at us."

The three of us look over at the same time. "Guys!" John hissed. "Don't make it obvious!"

We ignore him and keep looking at the table. He was right, there was a table surrounded by a small group of people looking our way while pointing and whispering. It made me a little uneasy.

"I wonder what their problem is," Lisa said, leaning back against her chair, crossing her arms over her chest and staring right back at them.

"Well, I'm about to find out," Terry said. He was up and out of his seat before any of us could utter a word to stop him.

We all turned in our seats to watch as Terry walked right up to the table. I secretly admired Terry. He never had a problem with confrontation, or going up to total strangers and introducing himself. He was an all-around friendly guy and everyone loved him. I know we certainly did.

I, on the other hand, absolutely hated it. I would rather light myself on fire than confront anyone. Friendly or not.

So of course my heart immediately began pounding in my chest when he turned around and motioned for me to come on over to their table. "You two are coming with me," I told John and Lisa, grabbing their hands and pulling them along with me before they could escape. I quickly looked at each and everyone's face that was gathered around the table, but I couldn't tell if what I was walking into was a good situation or a bad situation.

"Is this really you?" Terry asked as someone handed me a cell phone. Displayed on its screen was a picture of me and Camden, leaving his house together.

Shit.

I cleared my throat. "Yeah, that's me." I mean, there was no way that I could possibly deny it. The picture was clear as day, showing me walking out of my boss's house in the morning, with him by my side.

"So it's true then?" Someone else at the table asked. I looked, but I wasn't sure who they were. There were so many employees here at Luxmore Inc, it was impossible to know everyone.

"Is what true?" I asked, unsure if I really wanted to know or not.

"That you're sleeping with the boss."

I swear, everyone in the cafeteria heard them say that and stopped what they were doing to stare at me. At least, that's what it felt like in this moment.

I shook my head, letting out a pathetic attempt at a laugh. "No, absolutely not. I promise."

Yeah, pile on the denials, that'll convince them.

I took a deep breath. "You all know I'm his secretary and often pick him up for work in the morning. That's all this was," I said, referring to the photo.

"Oh, yeah," answered the girl on my right. I didn't know her name either. "I guess I forgot about that."

I forced a smile. "Well, I'm glad we got that cleared up. Where did you get that picture, anyway?" I ask.

"No idea," the owner of the phone shrugged sheepishly. "It's been circulating on our work's message forums. No name was posted with it."

Great. Yet another thing to deal with.

"Are you okay?" John asked, putting his arm around me.

"Of course," I answer. "Why wouldn't I be?"

Maybe because in addition to your house burning to the ground and having to live with your boss the entire place thinks you're now sleeping with him.

I needed a vacation. Far away from here.

We headed back to our table to finish our lunch as

quickly as possible. I didn't have any desire to stay in here a second longer than I absolutely had to. I could still feel everyone's eyes on me and hear their whispers and accusations.

As Lisa and I got back to our desk after lunch, Camden's office door opened so hard it bounced off the wall. Out walked Desmond, Camden's older brother. Lisa and I immediately looked at each other, eyes wide open.

What the hell? I mouthed. She just shrugged in reply. We knew who Desmond was. Well, knew of him. But no one has ever really seen him, besides the occasional function out of work. Certainly not *at* work. I also knew him and Camden didn't really get along so it was a little alarming seeing him here, storming out of his brother's office like this.

Lisa took a seat and I slowly made my way to Camden's office, knocking on the door before entering. "Be careful," she called out softly. I nodded, turning and taking a deep breath.

Everything appeared to be normal in his office. There was no upturned or broken furniture, no papers or books scattered about. Maybe it wasn't that bad of a visit after all.

"Everything okay, Mr Luxmore?" I ask, not

knowing what to expect. He was staring out the window but turned when he heard my voice.

"Fine," was all he said in reply. But his face gave him away. Whatever Desmond had said to him had left him fuming.

"Do you need anything?"

"No," he waved me away and walked over to sit at his desk. I nodded once before turning around to return to my own desk, wondering what the hell just happened.

Things at home that evening were no different. Camden hadn't said a word to me all the way home. Only speaking once we were inside. "Don't forget that tomorrow is the annual Luxmore get-together," he reminded me before disappearing into his bedroom.

I guess I was on my own for dinner again.

Chapter Eight

Each year Luxmore Inc held a huge get-together for all of their investors, business partners, family members, and any other person they deemed important enough. It was basically a time to come be with like-minded people, brag about your recent accomplishments, or use the opportunity to form new connections.

For the past eight years I have attended with Camden. I stayed by his side, following him throughout the night. Mainly, my job was to keep him company and make sure he steers clear of certain family members.

Namely Desmond.

For the first few years he attended, he remained on his best behavior. But as expected, that didn't last long. Something changed within him the past couple years.

He acts entitled to Camden's money, contacts, and his status. He thinks he's owed anything and everything, even though he hasn't lifted a finger to help out at the company. In his mind, just having the last name of Luxmore was enough to open all kinds of doors and opportunities for him. And that because of his name, he should never have to work for anything in his life.

Wealth, education, connections. They all are key. With all three of these, you can become a person that is feared.

And that is exactly what Desmond wanted.

He lacks the education part of the equation, though at no fault of his parents. Like Camden, he was placed in the most prestigious schools. His parents hired the best tutors that money could afford. They did everything in their power to get their children set up for success in life.

Camden excelled at both school and business. He studied harder than anyone I've ever known. Failure was simply not an option for him.

Desmond, on the other hand, screwed around, partying instead of attending to his studies. He figured his parents could just buy his grades. But that's just not how the world worked. That's not how Luxmore Inc worked. There were no shortcuts or handouts, as he was learning. Still, a part of him refused to believe this and was still in the mindset that someday, everything Camden had acquired would be his.

So my job tonight was to keep those two apart.

I hated it. But I stayed right next to Camden's side as he wandered around, greeting everyone. So far we had been here for an hour with no sighting of Desmond.

While Camden was deep in conversation with a potential investor, I took the opportunity to slip off to the bar for a glass of wine.

"Rough night?" A female voice asked as I took a healthy sip. I looked over at the owner of the voice and almost dropped my glass.

Monica.

"No, no. I'm having a great time," I said with a shaky voice. "I just needed a little breather."

Monica laughed, and I wished I could erase the sound from my brain. "An event like this would be a bit much for someone like you," she said, her voice dripping with condescension. I narrowed my eyes at her, never wanting to punch someone in the face more, but she didn't seem to notice.

"You know you'll never be with him, right?" she continued, and my eyes now widened. "He loves himself way too much, to the point where he can't ever be satisfied with others. And believe me," she leaned in closer to me, lowering her voice at the same time, "I have tried, over and over again," she said suggestively.

My heart dropped at the mention of her and Camden together. I didn't want him, not in the way she's suggesting, but it didn't mean I wanted to picture him doing it with anyone. Especially not with her. In my eyes, Monica Weaver was nothing more than a gold digging whore.

After dumping that lovely image in my mind, Monica smirked at me knowingly before pushing off the bar and making a beeline for Camden. I watched as she ran her fingers up and down his arm as he leaned in to listen to whatever she was whispering to him. For the next few hours she never left his side, her hands never leaving his body. It made me feel sick inside.

As I stayed near Camden, since it was my job to do so, I tried to distract myself from thoughts of the two of them together. My mind kept drifting to the beginning of the party, when I was the one by Camden's side. Earlier, I swear I felt little electric shocks every time any part of my body came in contact with Camden's. It left me both wanting more and completely confused.

He's my boss, there was no reason for me to feel this way.

On the other hand, it had been forever since I had

been touched at all by a man, so I convinced myself that's all that it could have meant. My body was just reacting to finally being touched, even in small, unintimate ways.

God, I was desperate.

But watching those two gave me the complete opposite feeling. I hated it.

I hated her.

I was going to need a whole lot more alcohol to make it through the night. I turned away from the two of them and back to the bartender, who would become my best friend for the night.

The rest of the evening went by in a blur. I remember walking around with Camden, hating on Monica, making friends with the bartender, and then not much else.

I woke up the next morning with a pounding headache. Why did I have to drink so much?

Then I remembered Monica's hands all over Camden, their closeness. I felt a pang of jealousy at those memories.

I sit up in bed, rubbing my head. It was not going to be a fun day at work. As I opened my eyes and my vision focused I had a moment of panic as I didn't immediately recognize the bedroom I was in.

Well, this isn't good.

Out of the corner of my eye I caught movement. Someone was in bed with me. Cautiously, I turned my head to see who was lying next to me and let out a gasp.

It was Camden.

I was in Camden's bed. What the hell happened last night? How drunk did I get? How drunk did *he* get?

I quickly look under the covers, my heart racing, to find that I was fully clothed. I was assuming he also was and I wasn't about to lift the blanket to find out. I could see that he was still wearing his dress shirt from last night. So it doesn't appear that we crossed any major lines last night.

I carefully snuck out of bed, trying not to wake him, and made my way to the kitchen for some water and aspirin. As I took the bottle out of the cabinet I vowed to myself to never get this drunk again.

"Can I get some too?" Camden grumbled, looking at the pills in my hand. I gave them over as well as my glass of water and got myself new ones. My entire face felt like it was on fire.

I avoided his gaze as I got a pot of coffee started. "So did anything . . ." I began, but never finished the question.

We both winced as Camden's cell phone went off. Why did that have to be so loud?

He hesitantly picked up the phone, putting it to his ear. "Hello, father," he spat, raising his eyebrows at me. I bit my lip in order to hide my laughter at his expression as I poured him some coffee and slid him the cup.

I sat down at the table as I drank the sweet caffeine, trying to give Camden at least a little bit of privacy.

He hung up after a few minutes, gulping down his coffee. "We should shower and get to the office as quickly as we can. My father will be meeting me there. It seems he has something important to discuss."

"What is it about?" I ask. His father never shows up at the office. Since Camden took over he never really felt it was necessary for him to be there as well. That's how much he trusted Camden with the company.

Camden shook his head. "He wouldn't say." he sounded angry. He set his empty cup in the sink and ran off to his room to shower without another word.

I soon followed, heading to my own room. Part of me, the part that was still a little drunk, kind of wished that we could be showering together.

It was definitely the still drunk part of me.

Chapter Nine

We arrived at the office and immediately everything felt off. Tension is weighing heavily in the air. On the way up to Camden's office, I noticed that it was eerily quiet. None of the usual morning chatter from the employees. Everyone was silent.

It gave me an uneasy feeling in the pit of my stomach.

I'm sure it had everything to do with the fact that Camden's father was meeting with him here today. It was something that never happened. Once his father stepped down and let Camden take over, he all but disappeared from the offices of Luxmore Inc. Which has been a huge relief for everyone working here. Camden may come across as a hard-ass sometimes, but he was nothing compared to his father. That man fired, berated, and made people cry like nobody's business. And often he did it because he was bored, or found it funny.

No one was sad to see him go.

So the change in the atmosphere must have meant that the devil himself had already arrived. I swallowed thickly. I hadn't spent much time around Walter Luxmore, apart from the annual get-togethers, but the man still made me nervous. I only started working for Luxmore Inc right after his departure, but I had heard the horror stories about him floating around the office.

We walked out of the elevator, down the hall, and as we rounded the corner to our offices, Lisa spotted us and stood up. "They're waiting for you in your office, Mr Luxmore," she shakily informs him, her eyes on the floor the entire time.

Camden nodded in response.

They? I assumed it was just going to be his father meeting him here.

I set my purse down on my desk and was ready to sit down when Camden cleared his throat. "Anna," he said, "I'll need you to attend this meeting with me."

My entire body tensed. Attending meetings with him is nothing new, it's something that I've done since first being employed here. There was just something about the way he said it that made me nervous. I look to Lisa, shooting her a silent plea to help me.

Sorry, she mouthed, with a slight shrug of her shoulders. I knew she was glad that it was me and not her having to face the senior Luxmore.

With a deep breath I followed Camden into his office. We walked in to find his father seated on one of the couches, with two men in suits standing directly behind him. I couldn't tell if they were bodyguards, lawyers, or what exactly they were. But they sure looked intimidating.

Seated beside his father was Desmon, looking at us with a smug smile planted on his face.

I could already tell whatever this was about was not going to be good.

"Come, sit," his father ordered, gesturing to the couch directly across from him. "But first, send her away," he nodded briefly towards me.

Camden straightened his suit jacket. "Not a chance. Anna has always attended every meeting with me. She's not going anywhere," he said firmly, his eyes never leaving his father's.

I have never wanted to leave a room faster.

"Very well," his father gave in after a moment.

I followed Camden to the couch and took a seat beside him, trying to avoid looking his father in the eye. This was already intense and I feel looking at the man directly would cause me to break down. The power that this man held was incredible. Untouchable.

And it made him absolutely terrifying.

"So what's this all about?" Camden asked, already losing patience.

His father quickly glanced at me, then leaned in closer toward his son. "We have a very important matter to discuss."

"And?"

He glanced at me once more, before shaking his head and continuing. "I guess I have no choice but to just come right out and say it." He cleared his throat and clasped his hands together. "I'd like you to get married."

Desmond smirked.

Camden laughed. "You can't be serious."

"Oh, I assure you I am. And let me rephrase that. You must get married. In one month's time. If you fail to do so you will be forced to step down as CEO of Luxmore Inc."

Well, that was unexpected.

"Wait. You're telling me I have one month to

marry or I forfeit my position? Is that correct? Am I hearing this right?"

"You are," his father said calmly.

"Everything I have worked for my entire life will be taken away if I don't give in to your ridiculous demands?" I could see the rage simmering in Camden's eyes. I've never seen him this angry before. "Why a month? Are you . . ." Camden suddenly straightened in his seat, his rage turning to concern. "Are you sick? Is this a living will type situation? I don't . . ."

His father waved off his concerns. "I'm not dying, if that's what you were getting at. I'm healthy as a horse. I'm just tired. So damn tired. I've been at this corporate game for quite some time now. All my life actually. And truthfully, I want to enjoy the time I've got left. Which is many, many years still," he held up his hand in protest of what his son might say. "But I want to make sure that all the bases are covered. Don't get me wrong, you have proven over the years that you are more than smart enough and capable of fully taking over the company. I have complete trust in you. The rest of the employees trust you as well."

Desmond sat next to his father, squirming and just generally looking uncomfortable as his brother was being praised by their father. I didn't know too much about Desmond, but I did know that he had his own little rivalry with Camden. He decided, in the past couple years, that he wanted to be the one to run the company. That he deserved the company. In his eyes, he was the perfect son.

It was a mess.

His father continued. "I just need to ensure that you marry a nice girl, one who can give us another heir to Luxmore Inc. I will not see everything I've worked for fall into the wrong hands," he said with murder in his eyes.

"But," his father shook his head, gathering himself, "this is something that simply must be done. There will be no negotiations."

"Have you ever known me to date anyone?" Camden asked. "I haven't so much as gone on a single date in years. All I have done is put my complete and total focus, all my energy into this company. Learning every single thing there is to learn about this company. So that I can efficiently and successfully run it. I have dedicated my entire life to Luxmore Inc. And now you come in here telling me that I have to get married, or I lose it all?" He asked, his anger growing by the second.

"Yes," his father answered calmly. "It's not enough

to merely know the ins and outs of the business nowadays. Showing everyone that you are capable as a businessman. No. Now, you must also prove that you are capable as a man. You must find someone you can hold an easy conversation with. Someone who can help sell the image of a stable marriage. Therefore, showing you as a stable man. That is how you win people over. That is what really attracts the investors. Being unmarried as a CEO can have a negative impact on a company. Think of it this way," he said, leaning forward in his seat, "marriage is more like a business transaction for people like us. It's a strategy that provides trust and security, for everyone involved. They don't believe in innocent love. Love, too, is a materialistic affair that is realized with profit in mind. A marriage is a crucial part in solidifying the CEO's position."

"And giving me a month to find and marry someone is the answer?" Camden raised his eyebrows in question. His face remained calm, but I could see his hands clenched in tight fists. The tension in the room began to make me feel uncomfortable, so I excused myself and stood off to the side, near the door. I had no idea why Camden insisted I remain here. This was the best I could do.

"It is," he stated matter of factly. "That's the timeframe I was given when I met and married your mother. Everything worked out perfectly for us. And the two of us are happier than ever."

Camden shook his head. "And you expect me to have the exact same results?"

"I don't see why you wouldn't," his father said, standing to signal the end of the conversation. "One month," he warned, holding up one finger to drive his point. "This is not up for debate. It's just the way things are done." He straightened his suit jacket and without another word, turned to leave Camden's office, followed closely by the two men in the dark suits. They hadn't said a single word the entire time they were here. I kept my eyes to the floor to avoid any uncomfortable glares from him.

Desmond got up wordlessly as well, stopping directly in front of me. I looked up to see his eyes slowly roaming over every inch of my body. It made my skin crawl. I caught his eye for a second and he winked before continuing his way out the door.

I let out a huge breath.

What a morning.

Camden paced back and forth. I know marriage has always been the last thing on his mind. Hell, even dating alone has been the last thing on his mind. I can't imagine what he's going through right now. Working for and eventually taking over Luxmore Inc has been all he's ever wanted. His entire life has been dedicated to this company. A wife and kids were never on the agenda for him.

I watched helplessly as he continued his pacing, not knowing what to say. How could you possibly comfort someone in this situation? He scrubbed his hands through his hair, muttering "What am I going to do?" over and over to himself.

The door to the office flew open. I looked up, expecting to see Desmond walking back in, instead to find none other than Monica Weaver.

Again. This woman just keeps showing up, unexpected and uninvited.

My blood boiled at the sight of her. Didn't she have anything better to do? I had to watch her latch herself on to and drool all over Camden last night. What could she possibly want now?

"Monica," Camden sighed. Seems he's just as happy to see her as I am. "What are you doing here?"

"Well, I came to see you, silly," she laughed. The sound reminded me of nails on a chalkboard. "Actually, I heard all about your father's ultimatum. And I have the perfect solution," she says as she draped herself over one of the couches.

Camden looked at her, hopefulness flashing across his face. "You do?"

Monica nodded her head, an excited look on her face. "Yes. You should marry me."

My heart stopped. Camden . . . marry Monica? No, I wouldn't allow it. He can't. She's absolutely crazy.

He just stared at her, and for a minute I feared that he might actually be considering it. Then he threw his head back and laughed. "Yeah, right," he told her.

She looked offended. "And why not? You know I'm perfect for you. I'm educated, I come from an established family. Unlike some people," she said, eyeing me with a look of disgust on her face. "I think we'd be perfect together. And I promise, I would be the perfect wife to you," she batted her eyelashes. She looked absolutely ridiculous.

Camden took a few steps closer to her. "I don't know where you heard about all of this, but it is none of your business. It's not your problem and I will never, ever marry you. Not even if I was forced to."

I could see the tears forming in her eyes from over here. I didn't feel bad for her, though. She didn't belong with Camden. She wasn't good for him.

"But," she began, but Camden waved off her protests.

"You and I will never be together. Never. And do you want to know why?" He leaned on the back of the couch. "It's because you're weak and incompetent. You're the type of person who, in order to protect themselves, does nothing but harm others. You care about nothing but yourself and you have nothing to offer me. Now, get the hell out of my office. You're not welcome here."

Monica looked like she wanted to say more, to beg and plead with him to change his mind, but instead grabbed her purse and stormed out. I had a feeling though that she was not about to give up.

Once I was sure no one else would be barging into the office I walked over to my boss. "Are you okay, Mr Luxmore?" I asked. It sounded pathetic, but I truly didn't know what else to say.

Camden shook his head. "No," he admitted. "I have no idea what I'm going to do. I can't lose everything I've ever worked for."

I sighed heavily. I knew just how much this job meant to him. I've been by his side for eight years now. This job was everything to him. "I wish there was something I could do to help," I whispered. I meant it. I would do anything for Camden. I hated seeing him like this.

"Me too," he said.

"Wait!" he said with a snap of his fingers. "Maybe there is something that you could do."

"What is it? I'll do anything."

He grabbed me by the shoulders, turning me so that I was facing him. He looked me straight in the eyes.

"Marry me."

Chapter Ten

I must not have heard him correctly. Being so close to Camden that I could feel the heat coming off his body, has made my brain all fuzzy. I couldn't concentrate or think clearly around him. There's no way that he just asked me to marry him.

"So what do you say?" Camden asked, an expression of hope mixed with desperation spread across his face.

"About what?" I asked, playing dumb.

Please say something other than 'marry me.' Anything.

He released my shoulders, taking a step back. "What do you say about us getting married? Think about it," he says, not giving me a chance to reply. "It's the perfect solution to both our problems."

I wasn't aware that I had a problem.

"We get married, I get to keep my position at the company, and you get the comfort and security of marriage."

The comfort and security of marriage? What about love? Did that factor in anywhere for him? He may not have wanted or believed in love, but some of us sure did.

"I . . . I think it's crazy," I admitted.

Camden looked shocked, as if he hadn't been expecting to be turned down. Which I suppose he wasn't. Camden Luxmore was a man who always got what he wanted. No one ever dared to tell him no.

"Crazy?" He demanded. "There's nothing crazy about any of this," he argued. "Come here," he said, grabbing my hand and leading me back over to the couches. I took a seat and he sat down opposite me. He took a few seconds, gathering his thoughts before continuing. "How long have you been working for me?"

The question caught me off guard. "Eight years."

"Eight years," he nodded in agreement. "So you should know me pretty well by now, yes?"

"Well, yes, but . . ." Where was he going with this?

Camden leaned forward, resting his elbows on his knees. "We have seen each other practically every day, every single day now for eight years. In those eight years I've never dated anyone and I haven't seen you with another man either. You know everything there is to know about me. It's almost as if you and I are already in a relationship with each other, wouldn't you agree?"

I shifted under his gaze. "I never thought about it that way." My cheeks burned with embarrassment. Had I really not dated anyone for that long? I searched my memory but came up with nothing. Not a single date.

Was I not dating because I truly had no interest or had I been far too busy with this job?

"As you know, I don't give myself to just anyone. In fact, I don't give myself to anyone, at all. Ever. You should consider yourself lucky."

I rolled my eyes at him. "You're so arrogant sometimes."

"Maybe," he said with a simple shrug of his shoulders. "But I have no problem speaking my mind. And I know what I want."

He can't be telling the truth. And he can't mean what I think he means.

Right?

There's no way in hell anyone even half as successful and attractive as him would want me. And certainly not Camden Luxmore himself.

This must be a cruel joke. Camden is known for being downright evil at times.

But I never thought he'd be like that with me.

I narrowed my eyes at him, crossing my arms over my chest. "You can't be serious." What in the world could have convinced him in these last eight years that I would ever want to marry him?

Camden looked at me, hesitating for a split second before speaking. "I've never been more serious."

I searched his face for any signs of laughter, a smile, anything to indicate that this is in fact all just a cruel joke. That, at least, I could deal with. But his expression remained serious.

"You've been by my side for so long, you know me so well. More than anyone else," he continued. "Why not you? I can't think of anyone better. Do you really have any other prospects? Do you really have any objections to the two of us getting married? We're together practically day and night as it is. Things really wouldn't be that much different. Nothing has to change," he argued. "Besides, we already live together. Isn't marriage naturally the next step?"

Yeah, if you were actually dating the person and in love with them.

My heart began to beat wildly in my chest. This conversation was crazy. He was crazy.

"One, I'm with you day and night because you constantly call on me. Me, and only me. You refuse to memorize anyone else's number. And two, we currently live together because my house was destroyed in a fire and I literally have nowhere else to go. Besides, it was your suggestion."

"Exactly. So you know it's a good idea."

I rolled my eyes in response. This man was infuriating.

Camden shifted in his seat, his determination unwavering though. "Don't you think you should be a little more grateful?" he asked, a little anger beginning to seep out of him. "After all, I did save you from having to live on the streets. So I think you owe me this favor."

"Favor?!" I yell, standing up to face him. "Is that all marriage is to you? A favor? A business deal?"

Camden sat back and shrugged, a look of indifference on his face. Now I was the one feeling angry. "So this is how you propose, huh? This is how the great Camden Luxmore proposes marriage to a woman," I huffed.

He threw his hands up in the air. "What do you want from me? It's not as if I've ever thought about marriage before. Hell, I barely even date. This was all just thrown at me."

"And I have to get dragged into this?"

He stands up, taking a step towards me, taking in a deep breath to calm himself down. "Look, this isn't an ideal situation, for either of us. But I can't think of anyone better than you. If I have to be married, I'd like it to be to you."

I'd like it to be to you. That's as close to a compliment as you're ever going to get out of Camden Luxmore. And I have to admit, that was almost romantic.

Almost.

He doesn't have a romantic bone in his body, that much I know is true. So what would marriage to him look like?

I'm crazy for even considering this.

"It's only marriage on paper," he says, his tone gentle. It's as if he could read my mind.

I caught the hopeful glint in his eyes, and my heart flipped. Camden's not the worst man in the world I suppose. And living with him has been surprisingly easy.

Maybe I really am crazy.

I suck in deep breath. "I'll do it on two conditions.

One, we keep it a secret, at least at work. No one here can know."

"Done," he nodded eagerly. "And two?"

"Two, you have to at least take me on some kind of date."

"A date?"

"Well, yeah," I shrug my shoulders, as if it was an obvious request. "You don't expect me to marry you without at least going to dinner, do you?"

He thought about it for a moment. "I think I can handle that," he says at last. Camden stuck out his hand and we shook on it.

What the hell was I about to get myself into?

Chapter Eleven

I still can't believe I agreed to do this. In just a couple weeks, I would be marrying Camden.

My boss.

"This . . . won't do," he says, roaming his eyes disapprovingly over my body. "You need new clothes. Actually, you need an entirely new wardrobe. You are about to become my wife. You should at least look the part."

The part. Just another reminder that this wouldn't be real. I always thought that I would be happy about my wedding day when the time came. That I would be excited to plan it with the love of my life.

But I'm not. I'm not happy and I'm not marrying for love. I'm marrying so that my boss can keep his position at the company.

This is so unfair.

A few days ago Camden informed me that every last detail of the wedding would be planned and taken care of by him. And all I'd really have to do is show up and look pretty.

Not quite the magical day I always thought it would be.

Yes, I was grateful not to have the stress that comes with wedding planning, but still. I at least wanted to help out a little. Maybe then it wouldn't feel quite as fake. It would certainly make it easier to at least pretend to be happy with this arrangement.

Camden was the only one that was truly benefitting from this so-called marriage. Without my help, he would pretty much lose everything. I would lose nothing if I didn't go through with this, if I didn't agree to Camden's 'proposal.' I also didn't stand to gain anything.

But here we were at a department store with names I couldn't pronounce, let alone afford to even walk into, so that he could dress me up like a doll. I had a few dresses and pant suits that I loved and thought were pretty decent, but they apparently make me look the complete opposite of what a billionaire's wife would look like.

After several hours of trying on clothes that cost

more than my house, Camden finally seemed satisfied with his choices. He had picked out everything from shoes to jewelry to the clothes itself. It cost more than I made in six months. Camden didn't seem to bat an eye as he handed over his credit card. I, on the other hand, nearly had a heart attack upon hearing the total.

"It's way too much," I half-whispered. "I don't deserve any of this." Even as just a rental. It felt wrong wearing a dress that cost more than what a monthly house payment used to be.

"Nothing's too much when it comes to you," Camden says, waving off my concerns. It was almost as if I was getting a glimpse of the softer side of him that I was sure he had but kept hidden way down deep.

Almost.

He slowly raked his eyes over my body. He had insisted that I wear one of the new dresses right out of the store as he has a date planned for us after this. "Now I'll have a hot wife," he says with a devilish look in his eyes.

"But I haven't answered you yet," I pointed out. I mean, I was doing this, but technically I hadn't given him a definite answer. I had told him that I wanted at least one date before I agreed to marry him.

Camden's lips turn up in a cocky smile. "No, but you will."

I scoffed. He was not making this easy. How was I ever going to make it through this?

He motioned for the workers to help load all the bags into his car. He then had his driver take them back to his house and gave him instructions on when and where to pick the two of us back up.

He turned back towards me. "The restaurant where we have a reservation is just down the street. I thought it would be nice to walk there," he informs me.

The place he chose was, in fact, just down the street. We walked in and the place was empty aside from the people working there. They nodded politely at Camden and guided us to a table overlooking the water. There were roses on the table next to some candles that gave off a soft glow. They also gave off false romantic vibes. If I was here with anyone other than Camden it would have been absolutely romantic.

And if this had been a real date.

But this really was just another sort of business deal for Camden. I was just here to play along.

"Are you sure this is okay?" I ask, looking around at all the empty tables and chairs.

"Of course. Why wouldn't it be?"

"There's no one here," I whisper. It felt wrong being here like this.

Camden didn't even look up from his steak. "That's because I rented out the entire place for tonight, so that we could have a private, peaceful time."

Oh.

We sat in silence as we ate. I didn't know what to say in this situation, as it wasn't a typical date. You usually use the first date to get to know a little about the person. But I know pretty much all there was to know about the man sitting across from me.

And it was clear that he wasn't interested in me other than to use me to secure his position at Luxmore Inc. So the only sounds for the first part of the evening were of our cutlery clinking against our plates. It would be nice if he would at least put a little bit of effort into this.

It was going to be a long night.

After we had finished our meal and the waiter took our plates, Camden wiped his mouth and sat back, staring out over the water. If this was any other date, any other guy I would say that I was lucky. The man sitting across from me was one of the most sought after in the city. Although I don't think he cared or was even aware of the fact. He could have had his pick of any woman.

My curiosity was getting the best of me. "So why

me?" I asked. There had to be at least a hundred women out there who would jump at the chance to marry the great Camden Luxmore. Certainly more fitted for the role than me.

He pulled his attention away from the water to finally look at me. God, this man was sexy. *No*, I internally scolded myself. This is not a real date, we can't be thinking of him like that.

"What do you mean?" he asked.

I cleared my throat, my nerves starting to get the best of me. "I mean, why me? Out of every woman you know, why me? I'm not suited to be your wife." Pretend or not.

"You're different from all the women."

I narrowed my eyes at him. "How so?"

"I actually like you," he answered simply, leaving it at that.

That was an answer I was not expecting. Heat crept up the back of my neck.

Camden studied my face for a minute before checking his watch. "Are you about ready to head out? We don't want to miss the second half of the date."

"Second half?" This was a surprise to me. I thought the restaurant was the extent of the date.

"Come on," he said, standing up and taking my hand in his.

The next thing I know I was standing in the middle of a yacht out in the middle of the river. The cool night air blew through my hair, whipping it all around. It was even more peaceful out here than in the quiet restaurant.

I smiled over at Camden, who had taken a seat in one of the squishy looking chairs. For once he actually looked to be somewhat enjoying himself.

"Thank you for this," I gesture to the yacht, "and for everything else tonight. It was perfect," I admit, moving to sit on the couch. It was like an entire living room set up here, and it was surprisingly comfortable.

"I'm glad you're enjoying it," he said, "but the night isn't over just yet."

As if right on cue, fireworks began exploding out over the water. Camden moved to sit right next to me.

"This is all for you," he said with a twinkle in his eye. "Sit back and enjoy it."

I truly had no words. I know this was a fake date, but it was the best damn date I have ever been on. And if this is how he does it for a fake date, the real thing has got to be extravagant.

Camden took off his jacket and placed it over my shoulders as I shivered. The night was beautiful but because we were out on the water it had gotten a little chilly. He placed his arm around my shoulders as well and I took the opportunity to lean into him.

We stayed this way as we watched the fireworks explode and the colors dance across the sky.

I turned to Camden, heart pounding. "Yes, I will marry you."

Chapter Twelve

I now had the unpleasant task of breaking the news to my sister. I was hoping Julia would be understanding of my situation. Still, I wasn't sure exactly how much I should tell her. We didn't really want too many people knowing of our arrangement, especially about the part of it being fake. That little piece of information definitely had to be kept locked up tight or else Camden could lose everything. His father was firm in wanting Camden to be married, and I doubt he would take too kindly to the news of his son entering into a fake marriage. That certainly wouldn't earn him any trust.

I decided to have her meet me down at the boardwalk instead of our usual restaurant. This way we could move around and go for a walk while I told her the news. I was much too nervous to be seated across from her right now. I don't think I'd be able to look her in the eye. My hands were already shaking and my heartbeat was through the roof.

"There you are," Julia's voice broke through my thoughts. I turned my attention away from the water and towards my sister. "Why are we meeting out here?"

I shrugged. "I just thought that a walk would be nice. The weather is perfect today." I shoved my hands into my pockets so she wouldn't be able to see my nervousness.

"It is beautiful out here," Julia agreed, leaning on the railing and looking out over the water. "I don't get to make it out here as much as I would like to with the kids. I can't even remember the last time I took a walk to just relax." She closed her eyes, taking in a long deep breath of the fresh air.

I now felt a little guilty about the fact that this was going to be the opposite of a relaxing walk. I took in a deep breath, deciding it would be best to just get this over with. If I waited any longer I'd lose the last bit of confidence that I had.

"I actually have some news," I told my sister.

She looked at me then squinted her eyes. "Good or bad?"

"Well that depends on how you look at it I suppose."

Julia shifted her body so that she was facing me, giving me her full attention. "All right, let's have it," she said, her voice gentle. I could see in her eyes that she was a little nervous about what I had to say.

"I'm getting married."

Julia laughed. "Married? What? Oh . . ." she stopped when she saw my face. "You're serious."

I nodded once.

"You're serious?" she asked, wide eyed. "How can you be serious? You're not even dating are you? I mean surely I would have heard about you seeing someone." She stared at me, her eyes demanding an answer.

But the truth was I still was unsure just how to answer. I will admit I came here today completely unprepared. I just knew I would have to tell her something. Julia wasn't only my sister but she was basically my best friend as well. And marriage isn't something you usually hide. I just had to bend the truth about it a little.

So lying it is.

I took a deep breath, feeling my body begin to shake with nerves. "I have been seeing someone."

Julia's head snapped up. "Seriously? Why haven't you said anything? Oh," her hand flew to her mouth. "Are you embarrassed about him? What's wrong with him? What can I do?"

Her questions were all over the place, but it was touching how concerned she was.

"Nothing's wrong with him," I laughed lightly. "We just wanted to keep it a secret is all," I lied easily. Heat crept up the back of my neck. I hated lying to my sister.

Her expression fell. "So there really is a man?"

I nodded.

"And you really are getting married?"

I nodded again.

"Well," she exclaimed, "Who is it who is going to be my brother-in-law?"

And there was the question I was really dreading.

"It's . . ."

"Is it someone I know?"

"Yes," I answered honestly. "It's Camden," I sighed.

Julia blinked a few times trying to process what I had just told her before responding. "Camden? As in Camden Luxmore, your boss?" She shook her head, not wanting to believe it. "Please tell me it's not him."

How many other Camden's do we know? "It's him." I looked down at my feet. I wasn't sure if I was embarrassed or ashamed. All I know is that I hadn't felt either of those things until talking to Julia.

"Are you out of your mind ?"she practically yelled.

This was exactly why I chose this spot to tell her, in case she got loud and made a scene.

"Julia, please calm down." I pleaded, looking side to side checking for anyone who might hear her. But we seemed to have the boardwalk to ourselves today.

"How can I calm down?" she asked, now pacing back-and-forth on the boardwalk. "My little sister just informed me that she's marrying her boss. How can he think this is okay? How can you?" She stopped to face me.

I had never seen her this mad before. I hated having to keep the real reason I was marrying him a secret from her. I wish I could just tell her right here and now, just tell her everything.

But would she understand? To be honest, I'm not even sure I understand why I'm doing it.

But I am. It's happening.

I grabbed my sister by her shoulders, forcing her to look at me. "It's fine. I promise you, I only hid it in the first place because of who he is, how powerful he is. We wanted the media and the gossips to keep their noses out of our relationship. It was the only way we could be together and actually enjoy it." The lie rolled easily off my tongue. She seemed to buy it though. Her shoulder slumped as some of the tension left her body.

"You still could've told me," she said, her voice barely a whisper.

"I know."

"I am your sister. You should have been able to trust me."

Tears began to prick at the back of my eyes. She's not wrong. We just couldn't risk it. "But I'm trusting you now," I added quickly, knowing that the damage has already been done. "No one else knows about the marriage. You're the only one I have told." I offered her a pathetic smile.

Julia backed up from me and looked at the ground for a minute before speaking. "I won't tell a soul if you insist on going through with this."

I pulled her in for a hug holding her tight. "Thank you," I whispered.

But instead of hugging me back she pushed me away, avoiding looking me in the eyes. "I won't tell anyone, but I also don't approve of this. Do not expect to see me at this wedding."

Before I could say anything else she turned on her heels and walked away.

The tears that had previously been unshed now streamed down my face.

Chapter Thirteen

I knew from the beginning not to expect too much from today, with it being a fake marriage and all.

But still ...

The wedding, if you could really call it that, took place a couple weeks after Julia had told me she didn't approve of it and would not be attending. I hadn't really heard anything from her since then beyond the occasional check-in text.

It broke my heart.

Even though this was a fake marriage, I still wanted to have my sister by my side. She was the only family I had left.

I was still holding out hope though that when I walked out of this dressing room, I would see her out there waiting for me. SShe didn't even have to smile or pretend to even be happy for me.

She just had to be here.

The actual ceremony was to be a small simple affair held in Camden's backyard. It was the perfect place to hold a wedding. Directly behind his house was a man-made pond with fountains spouting on either end. In the center of the pond was a square stone platform with smaller stone squares acting as steps that lead to the platform. This would be where we would exchange our vows.

There was a team of people here in my dressing room with me to make sure that I looked absolutely perfect for my big day. I briefly wondered if any of them knew that it wasn't real, not that they would be able to say anything anyway. I swear the wonderful lady doing my makeup had a look of pity in her eyes the entire time she was applying it.

I had wave after wave of emotion washing over me. I went from happy to sad to nervous. Everything in between. I felt it all.

Your wedding day is supposed to be a happy day. One of the happiest of your life, that's surrounded by friends and family. Filled with laughter and love.

Not this. This was nothing more than a business deal. Just another day for Camden. I've known him for eight years now, and I know he didn't believe in love.

But I did.

I still didn't know why I even agreed to go through with this. I wanted a real wedding someday. I wanted to fall in love with someone and to know that they loved me back.

Didn't I?

Honestly, I've never given it much thought over the years. I've been so busy with work and attending to Camden's every need. I've always been right by his side. The thought of another man had never entered my mind.

I shook my head, pulling in a deep breath. I can't be thinking like this now. I'm about to get married.

Fake married, but still . . married.

I ran my hands down the front of my dress, smoothing it out. I at least was allowed to pick out my own dress. It was pretty much the only real task I had today. True to his word, Camden did everything else. I didn't have to lift a finger to help.

I picked out a simple wedding gown with lace sleeves and intricate beadwork covering the bodice. It was light and airy and I will admit, I felt like a princess in it.

As I was admiring myself in the mirror a knock

came at the door. An older woman with a clipboard and a headset opened the door. "We're just about ready to begin," she informed me. She gave me a once over and nodded approvingly, closing the door without another word.

This is it, I thought, growing more nervous by the second. I was handed my small bouquet and I accepted it with shaking hands. Blowing out a slow breath to steady my nerves, I walked out of the dressing room, ready to become Mrs Luxmore.

I was led to the backyard where everyone was waiting for me. I quickly searched the small crowd, but found no sight of Julia. A huge part of me knew that she wouldn't change her mind about coming, but her absence still hurt.

I made my way to Camden, who was patiently waiting for me on the platform in the center of the pond. The way he looked right now took my breath away. Camden has never looked sexier.

The way he looked at me now is the way I always imagined my real future husband would, like he was the luckiest man alive. And it broke my heart all over again. When I got married I was supposed to be ecstatic.

I was supposed to be in love.

We exchanged our vows among a sea of floating

candles. It was short and sweet, and over before I knew it.

We climbed into the waiting limo and were whisked away to the reception, which was being held at one of his father's many private clubs.

We walked in and as I looked around I noticed that all the guests seemed to be the same ones that attend the Luxmore's annual get-togethers each year.

Yet another sign that this is just another business deal.

Apparently, at high profile weddings such as this it's customary for the bride and groom to receive envelopes of cash instead of regular gifts from a registry. Which I suppose made sense since everybody here probably already had everything they could ever possibly need. So they were just given more money to invest back into their businesses.

I stood next to Camden with a fake smile plastered on my face as I shook everyone's hands and accepted their congratulations. My feet were killing me and all I wanted to do was sit down and take my shoes off. I wore high heels every day for work, but I've never had to stand in them in one place for so long before. It was torture.

Other than my feet feeling like they were going to

fall off, it was all going fairly well until *she* stood right in front of me.

Monica.

I hadn't noticed her at first but my heart stopped once I looked into her eyes.

What the hell was she doing here?

"Congratulations," she smirked. She stuck out her hand and I stared at it in disgust for a second before hesitantly extending my own. She quickly grabbed my hand and pulled me forward causing me to stumble in my heels and almost fall.

I bet she would have loved that.

She leans in close and whispers in my ear. So close I could feel her hot breath against my ear. "You know this is all just temporary, right? You're just a fill-in and this cannot possibly be real. Camden and I are meant to be together, so you better watch yourself and stay the hell out of my way."

She released my hand and stood back, plastering a sickly sweet smile on her face before finally turning and walking away.

I let out the breath I had been holding. My heart was beating a million miles a minute. I didn't know if I should say something to Camden or not. I looked over at him, my husband, but he was happily chatting away with an older gentleman. He hadn't noticed our little interaction at all.

I decided not to bother him about it and to keep it to myself for the time being, and to at least try to enjoy the rest of the evening.

It went by without another incident, thankfully. Camden and I got home and I couldn't wait to change out of this dress. Walking into the house felt much different this time.

We didn't have any plans after the reception since there would be no honeymoon or anything. So I wasn't sure what to do exactly.

Were we going to sit together, maybe watch a movie? Have a late night dinner together? Go for a walk? I didn't know, but I felt like we should at least do something together. We did just get married after all.

I quickly changed into something more comfortable and waited for Camden in the living room. When he didn't come out of his room I went and knocked on his bedroom door, hoping that he wasn't asleep.

Some wedding night that would be.

"Come in," he called softly. I opened the door to find his suitcase and a few folded shirts sprawled across his bed.

My heart dropped.

He was packing.

"What's going on?" I asked, trying not to panic.

He answered without even looking up. "I have a business trip overseas."

"Right now?"

"I leave very early in the morning."

"Oh." Why wasn't I told? I usually attended these with him, being his secretary and all. I've done it all these years, never missing a single one.

Camden finally stopped, turning towards me. "I thought you'd like a couple days off, you did just get married after all."

Yeah, to you.

"This is all for you, by the way," he added, grabbing the silk bag from earlier that contained all of the cash given to us at the reception.

I opened it up and gasped. There must've been thousands of dollars in there. It was more money than I had ever seen in my life.

I shook my head. "I can't accept this, it's simply too much."

"Nothing is too much for my wife," he insisted.

His wife . . .

"Camden, I . . ."

He held up his hand to silence me. "One, now that we're married, call me Cam. At least in private. Two, I have no need for the money. Take it, use it as you wish.

And three," he set down the pair of pants he had been holding and stepped closer to me, "I should have said this sooner, but thank you for doing this. I know it wasn't an easy decision to make, and I'm not an easy man to be with. And I'm sorry that I have to go away so soon but," he straightened up, looking at me with an emotion I couldn't quite pinpoint, "take this time to relax. Enjoy the peace and quiet. You've been working so hard lately. You deserve it. I'll be home in a couple days," he said before resuming his packing.

I didn't know what to say. Real marriage or not, this was not at all how I envisioned spending my wedding night.

I quietly grab the silk sack of cash and walk to my room.

To spend my wedding night alone.

Chapter Fourteen

I hardly got any sleep that night, or the second night. All I could think about was how alone I felt. I didn't know what exactly would happen after we signed the marriage certificate, but this wasn't it. I guess I just expected him to . . . be here.

I know it was stupid of me to think that anything would change. That any part of this would feel real. I'm only hurting myself.

I barely left my bed yesterday. I have been married for almost 48 hours, yet I have never felt so lonely in my life. Camden was away on his business trip and I couldn't even call my sister for comfort. Her absence two days ago hurt more than Camden's did yesterday. I know Julia had said she wouldn't come, but I still held out false hope that she would change her mind.

I needed her then and I need her now.

My eyes wandered over to the silk money sack sitting on my dresser. I suddenly knew what I had to do.

It took me thirteen tries until Julia finally answered my call, and another hour until I had her convinced to finally meet up with me.

Choosing to sit in the corner of the coffee shop, I slid into one of the seats and sat down the 2 cups of coffee I was holding. I set my purse on the table and clutched the extra Chanel bag I had brought with me closer to my chest. I didn't get many gifts for the wedding, not that I was expecting any, but Camden's mother insisted I needed a few good bags. I picked one out as a sort of peace offering for my sister. Growing up she had always loved bags like this but we just can never afford one.

I hoped she would appreciate it.

It felt like an eternity before I saw her walk through the doors of the coffee shop. I grew more nervous as she made her way to my table. She sat down and I scooted the coffee I got her in front of her.

She took a sip and set the cup back down on the table, wrapping both hands around the cup. "So did you do it?" she asked, her eyes fixed to my left hand. "Did you actually go through with marrying your boss?" Her voice sounded even, so I couldn't tell if she was angry or not.

I quickly withdrew my hand, hiding it under the table. I don't know why I felt so ashamed all of a sudden. Camden and I didn't exchange rings, with his marriage not being real and us wanting to keep it as much as secret as possible.

"I did," I sighed. "I'm a married woman."

Julia's eyebrows raised in question but she didn't say anything else. Her silence was almost worse than anything she could've said in this moment. I should've at least gotten myself a cheap ring to wear out in public in times like this.

"I wish you would have changed your mind," I admitted. "I really wanted you there with me."

Julia said nothing, staring at her coffee. As she played with the cup I wished I was able to read her mind. I hated how uncomfortable it has become between us. Getting together with my sister has always been something I look forward to. Now all I wanted to do was get out of here as fast as I could and to the comfort of Camden's house.

Our house.

"I have something for you," I said before I lost my nerve and really did run out of here. Or before she did. She looked just as uncomfortable as I felt. I grabbed the Chanel bag and set it on the table in front of her. She stared at it for a few seconds, eyebrows raised. "A bag? Do you think your designer bag will fix everything?" she asked, her voice edged with anger now.

Well this isn't how I thought it would go. I knew she would still be a little upset about the entire situation, but I never expected this. Julia slid the bag back across the table. "I don't need this," she said, crossing her arms over her chest.

I swallowed thickly, trying to hold back the tears that were threatening to spill over. I slid it right back over to her. "Open it," I whispered.

Julia looked at me like she didn't trust me one bit, but did as I asked. She opened it and when she saw what was inside she quickly closed it up again. Her eyes darted around the coffee shop. She leaned in close, whispering, "Where did you get this?"

I had taken everything we had gotten from the wedding, all the money and put it in the bag for Julia. Her family needed it much more than I did. She had her husband and their four kids to take care of. I only had myself, and I truly didn't need much.

I leaned forward as well, taking Julia's hand in my own. "This was money we had received from Cam's business partners, family, friends, and other connections. We have no real use for it," I said, looking my sister in the eyes so that she would know that I was serious. "I want you to have this." She shook her head, opening her mouth to say something, but I cut her off.

"I really don't need it, I promise. Camden certainly doesn't need it." I let out a small laugh. "Take it, pay off what's left of our parents' debts, and then use the rest for your own debts. Use it for your family. Promise me that you'll use it to better your lives."

Julia had tears streaming down her face. "I don't know what to say." she whispered.

"Say you'll accept it. That you'll use it," I said, squeezing her hands harder.

"This is far too much," she began.

"It's not," I assured her. "It's more than enough to take care of all of the debt, and to take care of your children. I love you, Julia. I want to protect you. I want to help you, and this is one way that I can."

She walked around to my side of the table and sat down next to me, throwing her arms around me. "Thank you. Thank you so much," she cried on my shoulder.

"You're more than welcome," I answered, the tears now flowing down my face as well.

We sat there crying and holding each other for a while. Julia promised she would use the money wisely and that she would take care of everything. I believed her, and it felt so good knowing that everything was going to be alright. The debt that both of our parents had left us with and also the ones that she and her family had accumulated over the years were always weighing heavily on us.

It was like a huge weight had finally been lifted off my shoulders as I stepped out of the coffee shop.

I checked my watch and saw that it was getting close to the time that Camden would be getting home from his business trip. I wanted to be there when he arrived.

On the drive home I could feel myself growing more nervous the closer I came to the house. I wasn't sure how to act around him. Technically, he was my husband.

But at the same time he wasn't.

Chapter Fifteen

I pulled into the driveway and sat in my car for a few seconds, calming myself down before turning off the engine and stepping out.

"What the hell do you think you're doing?" A voice angrily called out. A car door slammed shut and my head jerked in the direction of the noise.

I was more than shocked to see Monica walking down the driveway towards me. Of course she knew where Cam lived. That fact made me really uncomfortable.

"I asked you what the hell you were doing?" She asked again, stopping directly in front of me.

My heart was pounding in my chest, and I was hoping she wouldn't be able to see how much her presence affected me. "What do you mean?" I managed to ask. Was she talking about me being here at Camden's? If so, I could ask her the same thing.

She stood back, putting her hands on her hips. "Just how is Camden going to feel now that you're handing out his money like it's nothing?" She asked, tapping her perfectly polished fingers impatiently on her hips.

How the hell did she know about the money?

My heart began to pound even harder. I could feel my palms beginning to sweat a little as well.

"You're going to ruin him, you know," she said, ignoring the fact that I hadn't even answered her in the first place. "I told Camden years ago that he needed to let you go. That you were no good. And here you are, proving me right," she said with a smug look on her face.

I knew I should say something, anything to clear this up, but my throat was dry from nervousness. Being out here in the dark with Monica was not my ideal situation. I had no idea what she was capable of. I had no idea when Camden would be home either and I wouldn't even know who to call for help. The closest neighbor was a little over a mile away. It was one of the main reasons Camden had purchased this house. He loved the privacy it gave him.

Right now I hated it.

Monica took a step closer to me. I stepped backwards, almost falling over, but before she could say or do anything else another car flew down the driveway.

My first thought was that Monica had back up for whatever she had planned for me. But as the car screeched to a halt and the door flew open I let out a sigh of relief.

Camden walked out of the car and straight over to my side. "Are you all right?" he asked me. I nodded, never happier to see him than I am right now. He turned his attention to Monica. "What's going on?" he demanded.

Her face quickly changed from the angry she-demon I had witnessed earlier to concerned. "I was just protecting you," she pouted, raising her right hand and pointing at me. "While you were away your *secretary*," she spat the word out like it had left a bad taste in her mouth, "has been stealing from you and spreading your money out all over town," she lied.

Camden put his arm around my waist, bringing me closer to his side. "I assure you that's not what she's doing," he told her.

She looked back-and-forth between the two of us and I could tell she wanted to rip us apart. "But she did. I saw her with my own eyes." She stomped her feet as she said this, and I couldn't help thinking that she looked like a child having a temper tantrum right now.

"You saw her with your own eyes," Camden repeated. She nodded eagerly, excited at the thought that she might be getting me in trouble.

"How did you happen to see her?"

"Well I followed her," she answered quickly. "I had a feeling that she was up to no good while you were away, so I followed her all today." She shrugged, like it was no big deal. No big deal that she had been invading my privacy this whole time.

Camden moved his hand to my back and began to rub it, seemingly sensing how scared I was. I leaned into him for comfort.

"So let me get this straight. You followed her around all day. Then came back here to what? Threaten her?" Monica opened and closed her mouth several times, not knowing what to say. I'm sure she has been hoping and counting on Camden to be furious with me and fire me on the spot. "I already knew what she was doing with the money," he continued. "She had called me earlier to tell me what she wanted to do with it and even asked for my permission. I loved her idea. It shows that she has a bigger heart than I thought possible. Besides, that money is my wife's and she's free to do with it as she pleases. It's absolutely none of your business what happens to it."

Monica's eyes went wide at the mention of his wife. She looked at me, staring with her eyes wide open, tears forming in them. I swear, I could pinpoint the moment when her heart shattered completely.

I can't say that I felt sorry for her.

"You need to leave," he told her sternly. "Don't ever let me catch you on this property ever again. You are no longer welcome here."

"But Camden . . ." she cried.

"Leave," he growled.

She hesitantly turned around and got back into her car. Camden didn't say another thing until she was out of sight.

"Are you sure you're okay?" he asked, his hands placed on my shoulders while he looked me over for any possible sign of an injury. His eyes were filled with worry.

"I am now," I said. I wasn't but he didn't need to know that. I was so glad he was back.

"I'm sorry that you had to deal with that," he said once we were safely inside the house, and I was seated in the living room. He handed me a cup of tea and took a seat beside me. It was strange having him make me tea and comforting me when I was usually the one making the tea in these situations. I don't know if I will ever be able to get used to it.

I just smiled and sipped my tea. I was still too shaken up from my encounter with Monica to trust myself to speak. We sat in silence for a while. It was comforting having him next to me.

After a few minutes, I finally became aware of just how late it was, and I started to yawn.

"I should let you get to sleep," Cam said softly. He picked up the tea cups and walked back to the kitchen.

"You too," I said suddenly. "You must be exhausted from your trip." It had completely slipped my mind that Camden had just flown back from overseas. "I'm so sorry to keep you up like this. I feel awful."

"Hey," he grabbed me by the shoulders, "there's no need to be sorry. We both had quite the eventful day," he chuckled.

I laughed. He had no idea just how eventful. Either way, we should both go get some sleep. After all, we both have to work in the morning.

"Anna," he said, stopping me as I got to my bedroom door. I turned to look at him. I don't know why but hearing him say my name like that felt . . . intimate. "Let me make it up to you."

"What do you mean?" I asked, genuinely confused.

"This whole weekend - the wedding, leaving you alone on our wedding night, having to deal with Monica. I know none of it was easy. And I have been pretty insensitive about it all. Let me make it up to you. Next weekend, I'm all yours. I'll plan everything," he said, causing my heart to skip a beat.

The thought of having him all to myself for a weekend had me excited. It was more than enough to make up for this crappy, disappointing weekend.

Chapter Sixteen

The following weekend Cam made good on his promise to make things up to me. He managed to whisk away for a full night together.

It may only be for one night, but I intended to make the very best of it.

We drop our bags off at the hotel after checking in and decide to go for a walk. Cam grabs my hand and I look at him in surprise. "No one here knows who we are," he explained. I guess I hadn't thought of that. "I promised you a romantic time so let's use the weekend to pretend like we're a real married couple."

I smile at him, though my heart breaks a little. I hated all the constant reminders that what we had isn't real, and never will be. I hated being married to a man who only saw me as a mere business transaction.

But I smiled anyway, determined to at least have a decent time. I never had the time or the money to travel on my own, so I may as well take advantage of this and try to enjoy myself.

We spent the next few hours walking up and down the bustling streets, admiring the architecture and the views. Dotted along the streets were stalls of street food, which had my mouth watering. I convinced Cam to stop at a few and try out the food with me. I had never tasted anything so amazing in my life.

We stopped in each little shop we found along the way, and we watched the many street performers. I had never seen so many people out and about in one place. Each street that we turned onto seemed more crowded than the last. Cam snaked his arm around my waist, pulling me in closer to him as we weaved our way through the crowds.

Once the sun began to set we found a rooftop bar with a breathtaking view of the city skyline. I settled in close to Cam, relishing the feel of his body against mine as we sipped our wine and watched the city lights come alive in the night. The cool breeze blew by, and I closed my eyes, taking in a deep, cleansing breath. I melted into Cam's side, feeling truly relaxed for the first time in a long time.

Away from the stress of work and having to hide

our marriage, not having to lie to anyone, I finally felt like I could breathe. We didn't have to sneak around, to lie. There were no pressures of any kind here.

We could just . . . be.

After a few glasses of wine we decided to take a walk along the beach. Holding my heels in one hand and the hem of my skirt in the other, we walked along the water's edge. Cam stayed on the dry sand, but I wanted to dip my toes in the water.

"You look so beautiful," Cam said as we were looking out over the water. I looked over at him, surprised by his sincere compliment. The moonlight cast different shadows over his face, but also gave him a certain glow.

He looked absolutely irresistible right now.

I turned away, swallowing thickly. I shouldn't be having thoughts like this.

But then Camden grabbed my chin, tilting my head up so that I was looking him in the eye. He moved until he was standing directly in front of me. Slowly, he leaned down until his lips brushed over mine. A small gasp escaped my lips.

I felt him smile against my lips as he lowered his face all the way down. He grabbed my waist, pulling me closer until our bodies were flush against one another.

I stood on my toes, weaving my hands through his hair as I deepened the kiss. My head spun, but I wasn't sure if it was from the kiss or from the wine.

Cam pulled back and looked at me, his breath ragged. "Do you want to go upstairs?" he asked.

I only nodded, not trusting myself to speak.

We got back to the hotel room and Cam carried me to the bed. He set me down and kissed me. Soft and delicate at first, but it quickly turned harder, more intense. Full of need and want.

Before I knew it Cam pulled back, resting his forehead against mine. Letting out a slow, pained breath he asked, "Are you sure you want to do this? Knowing that you and I aren't real, that our marriage isn't real? Is this," he gestured to us and to the bed, "something you want?"

My heart broke at his words, but I couldn't deny it. It was absolutely something I wanted. Real or not, I wanted Cam. All of him.

I nodded and he took off his shirt, discarding it on the floor. I took the opportunity to run my hands over his chest and abs. Looking up, I could see the desire in his eyes. I crushed my mouth to his.

Cam wrestled out of his pants and I slipped my sundress over my head, leaving me in only my panties.

Cam's eyes roamed hungrily over my body. "So sexy," he growled.

He ran his fingers over my opening. "Already wet, I see."

"Only for you," I said breathlessly.

Cam moved the fabric aside and slid one finger inside me, while using his thumb to rub circles over my already swollen clit. The sensation was already almost more than I could handle.

"Please Cam," I beg. "I need you."

He wasted no time in ripping the lace of my panties and tossing them to the floor. He repositioned himself at my slick entrance, glancing up at me for permission.

"Please," I begged.

Cam sunk deep inside me, holding still as I adjusted to his size. I moaned against his lips, already wanting more. I arched my back eagerly, and he takes that as his cue to slam into me over and over again. A thousand different sensations crash through my body, each one better than the last.

It didn't take long before Cam erupts inside of me, and we ride the waves of pleasure together. My muscles contract around him, and after one final satisfying thrust he convulses above me.

We collapse on the bed together, panting. I roll

over and curl up into his body. He wraps one arm around me and holds me close, planting a kiss on my head.

After a few minutes Cam's breathing becomes quiet and even. I checked to see him sleeping softly beside me. Carefully, I get up out of the bed, covering him up with the sheet.

I quietly walked to the bathroom and turned on the shower to drown out my sobs. Tonight was even better than I could've ever imagined, but now that I've had a taste of what a real relationship with Cam could be like ,how can I go back to merely pretending?

How could I keep my distance when all I wanted to do was be near him?

I hated this. Hated myself for agreeing to go along with this. All that I was going to get out of this entire situation was heartache, yet I wholeheartedly agreed to it.

I know it was stupid and selfish to want anything more and to dare to hope. But I had let myself go there.

To dare.

To hope.

My heart ache was no one's fault but my own.

I stood in the shower for longer than I intended to as it washed away my tears. Stepping out into the bedroom, I looked at Camden, who was still sleeping peacefully.

After the day we just had there was no way I was going to be able to give up. Once my tears ran dry and the shower washed away most of my doubt, I promised myself that I would at least give us a shot. I've known Camden for years and there's no way he would have treated me the way he did today if there wasn't maybe a small part of him that had feelings for me. Even if it was hidden deep beneath the surface.

I got dressed and climbed into the bed beside Camden, careful as not to wake him up. I laid down and went to sleep, determined not to give up.

Chapter Seventeen

After the semi-romantic weekend Camden and I had just spent together, concentrating on work had been nearly impossible. I now had a glimpse of what a real relationship with him could be like, and I wanted so much more.

I wanted him to look at me with the same possessiveness in his eyes that I had seen. I want to laugh with him, to spend time with him, doing anything but work.

I wanted him to touch me.

"Anna, come here, you need to see this," Terry whispered, breaking me out of my thoughts. My face grew hot and I hoped he wouldn't notice and ask why. Terry lived for gossip.

I found him hiding behind the wall that separated

my desk with their shared office. He was gesturing for me to follow him, all while keeping a watchful eye on Camden's door.

I followed him to their office where John and Lisa were hunched over an iPad, whispering feverishly in hushed tones. They gestured me over to them once they saw me with Terry.

"Have you seen this?" Lisa askedas John turned the screen around so I could see what they were looking at.

There, covering the screen was a picture of me with Camden. He had his arms around me, holding me close as he kissed the side of my head. I was practically sitting in his lap. Thankfully, my face was hidden behind my hair, which has been blowing all over the place due to the wind.

My hand flew to my mouth. "Oh, my God."

"I know, right?" Lisa asked, her voice low. "Who would've thought that Mr. Luxmore was seeing someone?"

"It's too bad you can't see her face though." Terry pouted. "I really wanna know who it is."

Terry turned his attention back to me. "What about you?"

My stomach dropped. I had to admit, you could kind of tell that it was me from that angle, but only if you look really closely. "What . . . I . . ." I stammered, unsure of what to say. Would they hate me if they found out I had a romantic weekend away with the boss? Would they hate me even more for the fact that I kept it from them? And oh, God, the rest of the company? The rumors that would fly . . .

Would I be fired?

"Well?" Terry pushed. "Do you have any idea who it could be?"

Lisa chimed in, face lit up at the possibility of gaining personal information on our boss. I tell you, these three live for gossip. "Yeah, you work closely with him. Has he ever said anything to you? Or have you seen him with a woman?"

Oh. I let out a long sigh of relief. They thought I had answers, not that I was the one in the picture. I cleared my throat, shaking my head. "No," I answered, " I have no idea who that could be. I didn't even know that he was dating. We don't talk about anything personal like that, only work," I quickly added, noting how John was kind of giving me the side eye. I really hope he didn't suspect anything. I hope they all believed me.

Terry picked up the iPad, flipping through the many pictures and articles already circulating. "How could they not get her face?" he complained. "Not one single face picture. This is huge news, you think they do a better job."

I slipped back to my desk as the three of them continued to debate about who they thought the mystery woman could possibly be.

They were pictures. There were articles. And it seems there were rumors and speculations already running rampant through the office. How could we have been so careless? Paparazzi and journalists were always lurking around, always on the lookout for the perfect photo and newsworthy mishap of the rich and powerful. Camden had a few that have stalked him regularly, for years. Waiting for the perfect story to bring his downfall. No doubt hired by Desmond, of all people. He wanted his brother's position and power so bad, I wouldn't put it past him to be the one behind this.

But still, we should have known. We should have been more careful.

By lunchtime the entire building was buzzing with the news that Camden was seeing someone. For as long as I have worked here, no one had ever seen him with a woman outside of work functions. So of course it caught everyone's interest, and everyone was talking about it.

The cafeteria was packed with people analyzing the

paparazzi photos, coming up with their own theories about who the mystery woman is draped over their boss. So far the guesses had been celebrities, politicians daughters, basically anyone rich, famous or powerful.

Someone the complete opposite of me.

That fact made me feel slightly better as I was nowhere near the status of any of these women. I'd be able to fly under the radar completely undetected. Nobody would dare guess that it was me.

But still, I felt a pang of guilt in my chest. I really hadn't thought that our weekend away could cause any sort of trouble for Camden.

I felt even worse sitting here with Lisa, John, and Terry as they made up their own theories. To not draw any suspicion to myself, I had to participate in the discussions. It hurt to imagine Camden with any of these other women, because let's face it, any one of them would be a much better match for him than I was. They all had much more in common with him.

And besides, I was only temporary.

After lunch I slunk back to my desk, in a worse mood than before. Even though Camden and I were married, it wasn't real. And I just spent an hour listening to a room full of people discussing scenarios that potentially could be true in the future. Camden could leave our fake marriage when the time is right and end up with any one of them.

And where would I be? Heartbroken and miserable.

Now all I wanted to do was cry. I had started this week off on a high from the weekend, but today has only been one big reminder that my happiness was all an illusion.

As I was sitting here feeling sorry for myself, Camden buzzed for me. I took a deep breath and stood, smoothing my skirt the best I could. I had to pull myself together. There was work to be done.

"You called, Mr. Luxmore?" I asked as soon as I entered his office. Calling him that felt strange, wrong even, after the weekend we just had. It was an odd feeling to be so formal with someone you had just seen naked.

"Yes," he said, gesturing me over to his desk. I walked over and stood in front of it, leaving the large oak desk to separate us.

Camden set aside the papers he had been looking over and leaned forward on his desk, clasping his hands together. He looked me straight in the eyes, something he never did. Usually when we spoke at work he hardly looked my way. Not out of rudeness or disrespect, but because he's always so busy, or we were walking through the building or something.

There's always one million things going on here at once.

"Are you okay?" he asks. I don't know what I'm more shocked about - his question, the gentle tone in his voice, or the concern for me that I see in his eyes. This isn't the same Camden Luxmore that we all know and tolerate.

"I'm fine," I said after a long minute.

Camden squinted his eyes and just looked at me, as if to say that he knows I'm lying.

"I was just informed of the news articles. I took a walk through the building and got wind of some of the rumors already circulating. So I'll ask you again. Are you okay?"

This was not what I was expecting him to say. I was hoping that the rumors wouldn't have made their way to him. People are usually pretty good about keeping the gossip down around him. Everyone knows how much Camden couldn't stand it. But I suppose this topic was just too much for some to keep quiet about.

I don't want to lie to him, but I also don't want to let him know just how much it all affected me. Just how awful it made me feel about myself. But I also knew he wasn't going to let this go.

I sigh heavily. "I've been better," I finally admitted.

"Come here," he demands, and I walk around his

desk. When I got close enough he grabbed my hand, pulling me onto his lap. It caught me off guard and I gasped as I landed on him.

"Someone could see us," I said in a panicked whisper.

"No one's going to come in here, not without my permission," he whispered into my hair. Which was true. No one dared to even put their hands on his office door without his permission. To make me feel better, Camden pushed the button on the side of his desk, the one that shut the blinds closed to his entire office.

But still, my coworkers were just on the other side of that wall.

As Camden held me tightly I could feel him hardening against me. "You know I'll always protect you," he says. I know he's just talking about the rumors floating through the office, but a part of me pretends it means something else entirely.

"I know," I said on a sigh.

"All I want right now is to rip all of your clothes off, right here in the office. I want to throw you down and kiss every last inch of your body, while anyone passing by the office listens, wishing they were us."

I'm breathless at his confession. My heart begins beating wildly.

He continued. "I fantasize about you on your knees in front of me as I sit at my desk. I've longed to bend you over this very same desk," he says, threading his hands through my hair. His warm breath on my ears sends chills up my spine.

I move my head so I can look him in the eyes. His gaze is full of desire. Without a second thought I lowered my lips to his, kissing him hungrily. Camden let out a groan as he pressed himself against my leg. I don't know how it's possible, but he's gotten even harder.

Camden lifted me up out of his lap and onto his desk. I eagerly spread my legs for him as he positioned himself in between them. I wrap my arms around his neck and pull his face to mine. Camden places one hand behind my head and with the other he finds my entrance.

"God you're so wet already," he growls. It's amazing what this man does to me. In one swift movement he had removed my panties and thrown them on the floor.

He undid his pants, slipping them and his boxes down as far as he could get them. He hiked up my skirt so my bare ass was sitting directly on his desk. He repositioned himself in between my legs.

I scooted myself closer to the edge of his desk and,

wrapping my legs around him, pulled him as close as I could as he sinks deep inside me. I had to bite his shoulder to keep from crying out as he filled me up. I wrap both my arms around him as he thrusts into me hard and fast, like he couldn't get enough of me.

It doesn't take long before we're both out of breath and completely satisfied. Camden pulls out, leaning his head down to rest his forehead on mine.

"We shouldn't make this a habit," he panted. "But I couldn't wait until we got home, I needed you. Bad."

"The feeling was mutual," I smiled up at him.

We quickly got cleaned up and erased any evidence of what had just transpired in his office. I planted a quick kiss on his lips before sneaking out of his office.

"Oh Anna," he called softly before I closed the door. "Don't forget, we have dinner at my parent's house tonight."

I nodded, before closing the door and taking a seat at my desk. I don't know how I was expected to get any work done after that.

Chapter Eighteen

I was nervous stepping into Camden's parent's house. I've met his father a couple of times during work functions, but I've never interacted with him outside of those situations before.

Camden was a powerful man, but his father was even more so. That fact alone had me practically shaking in my heels.

We get to the dining room and the first person I see is Desmond, seated next to his father. They were talking about something serious, judging by the looks on their faces.

They stopped once Camden's mother noticed us and exclaimed in an excited voice that her baby had finally arrived. I felt Camden's body tense. He absolutely hated it when his mother referred to him as her baby. He would always argue that he was a full grown man.

I could certainly agree with him on that.

As Camden gave his mother a quick hug I glanced at Desmond, which proved to be a mistake. Desmond slowly slid his eyes down the entire length of my body and back up again. He licked his lips, looking me directly in the eye. It made my skin crawl. But I put on the best fake smile I could muster and took a seat next to Camden at the table.

"I'm so glad you could make it," his mother said to me. Her smile seemed very genuine and helped to ease my nerves a little.

"Yes, indeed," his father added in a tone that stated he really thought otherwise.

The man had only said two words so far and I'm completely intimidated by him already. Camden must have sensed my unease as he brought his right hand down under the table, taking my left hand in his. He held it firmly, stroking the top of my hand with his thumb. That simple gesture alone helped me a lot. It also had another effect on me. It's amazing just how much a small touch like that could fill my entire body with need. I wondered if he knew the power he had over me.

Desmond and his father resumed their previous

conversation as we ate. His father wasn't entirely engaged in the conversation though, staring at me with hatred filled eyes instead. No one else seemed to notice though. As Desmond was concentrating on whatever he was discussing with his father, Camden and his mother chatted away happily.

I stayed silent, pushing food around my plate with my fork, feeling the weight of Mr. Luxmore's stares. I've never felt so uncomfortable in all my life. I couldn't wait to be at home where I could be alone with Camden.

Once everyone had finished eating and the table was cleared, his father leaned forward, clasping his hands together and resting them on the table. "So," he began, looking back-and-forth between me and Camden. The look in his eyes was one of disappointment. "We never discussed this marriage between the two of you."

My heart stopped at those words. Here it was, when his parents voiced their disapproval of me. Where they would throw me out and demand that their precious son marry someone of their status. I am nobody after all.

I felt sick all of a sudden. Camden put his arm around the back of my chair, stroking my shoulder with his thumb. I don't know if he was trying to reassure me or anything, but it really wasn't working. I know we weren't in a real relationship, but I still didn't want to lose him. Camden meant more to me than I had ever expected him to.

If they forced us to divorce, what happened to me? To my job? Would I be forced to resign? I loved my job. In all the years I've worked there, I've never once wanted to quit.

I wish I had never come to this dinner.

Camden eyes his father. "And what about it?" He stopped stroking my shoulder. Instead he placed his whole hand over my shoulder, pulling me in closer to him, as if to say that I'm not going anywhere.

"I'm sure you're aware," he began, "that she was not our first choice for you as a wife," he gestured to me with disgust in his voice. "Or even a choice at all."

Ouch.

I couldn't help but notice Desmond sitting there, looking smug with a smirk on his face.

"She's below you Camden, in every way." Nothing about that statement was wrong, but it still hurt like hell to hear.

I could feel Camden's anger at his father as he gripped my shoulder harder. Desmond's smugness only increased. I chose not to look over and see how his mother was reacting to all of this. I didn't want to add to the immense pain I was already feeling. She had been so warm and inviting to me since I first arrived at their house. I didn't want to shatter that illusion of her.

"I don't care about that," Camden nearly exploded. "She's my wife. I chose her. I chose her for who she is, not for her status or her wealth or any of that. I don't care about any of that shit. None of it matters to me."

If possible, I just fell harder for the man I'm not supposed to be in love with.

His father's features softened and he no longer looked like he was filled with pure rage. "I know, son," he said.

"You . . ." Camden said, looking just as confused as I was.

"Yes," his mother chimed in for the first time. She looked over at me with a warm smile on her face. "I will admit, you weren't at all who envisioned with our dear Camden," she said as she reached across the table to take my hand in hers. "But you have proven to be worthy of our son. I don't recall ever seeing him this happy before," she smiled at Camden, who had a confused look on his face. "Therefore, I believe this marriage can be good for him. For us."

I had no idea what that was supposed to mean.

Were they truly accepting me with Camden? I know it shouldn't, but it made me feel a little giddy, knowing that they thought I was someone who was good enough for their son.

Camden opened his mouth to speak, but Desmond beat him to it. He jumped out of his chair, causing it to move backwards and scrape against the floor. "Nothing I have ever done has earned me the approval of the two of you. But he," he pointed angrily at his brother, "gets to marry the help, and all is fine? Where is the logic in that? How is that fair? How was any of this fair?"

"Desmond, honey," his mother pleaded, but he ignored her as if she wasn't there.

"I have tried my whole life to get them to see me the way they see you," he spat. "Nothing I ever did was good enough. It seems it never will."

"That's enough," Camden warned. But Desmond was just getting started.

"Why? Do you want me to say that I was envious of you? That you were better at everything? That you had the best of everything?" He was pacing back and forth now, his body shaking from anger.

"No, I don't," Camden said, in a much calmer voice than I could've mustered. "I want you to stop this ridiculousness. Everything was certainly not handed to me. If I ever happened to have the best of anything, it's because I worked for it. Unlike you, I have worked my ass off, day and night, dedicating my life to this company."

"Obsessed much," Desmond sneered.

"No. Passion. I am passionate about this business. About this company. That's the difference between us, Des."

With that comment, Desmond leapt across the table, punching Camden directly in the face.

His mother screamed, and the two of us backed away from the table as fast as we could. I nearly tripped over my chair as I was trying to get away from the fighting that was happening. Their father raced around the table to comfort his wife while his oldest son pummeled his younger brother.

"Stop!" I cried, feeling helpless. Desmond didn't stop though, didn't even hesitate as he kept punching Camden. All the while Camden didn't fight back, not even once. He had been knocked to the ground and Desmond leapt on top of him. Camden just held his arms up in front of his face to take most of the blows.

"I'm so sick of you getting everything you want," Desmond yelled in anger. "Everything that should be mine has been cruelly handed to you. It's not fair," he said in between blows.

He paused his assault for a minute and stared down at Camden, his face twisting a bit. "Did you know that while everyone thought you and Monica were so in love, that she was coming to me to be satisfied? Guess you weren't enough of a man for her," he smirked, thinking that it would cut his brother deep. That Camden had ever really cared for her. "While she was supposed to be with you, she would be in my bed every night, screaming my name."

Camden still didn't say a word, which earned him a few more hits from his brother. All of a sudden Desmond stopped, snapping his head up to look in my direction. "You know," he said, panting from all of the effort of his assault. He raised his hand and pointed at me. "I think I'll just take her instead, just like I took Monica."

That comment seemed to set Camden off. He hauled off and threw one singular punch, knocking Desmond off of him and onto the floor. He grabbed his cheek and looked at his brother like he couldn't believe what just happened. Camden bent down near Desmond's face as he tried to back away. "There's no way in hell you will ever take my wife. She's the only woman I've ever loved. And she's not yours to take. You will never be with a woman half as good as her."

The only woman he . . . Did he really say that?

Everyone seemed as shocked as I felt. Even if just in anger, Camden Luxmore just admitted that he was in love.

I'm surely getting ahead of myself, but maybe, just maybe this could be the start of something real between us.

Or maybe I was being a complete idiot for hoping.

Camden turned to me and I cried at the sight of him. He already had bruises forming on his beautiful face, and there was blood near the corner of one of his eyes. I rushed into his arms and he wrapped them firmly around me, stroking my hair as I cried into his chest. "I'm okay," he whispered, over and over.

His father escorted Desmond out of their house, exchanging harsh words with him. Camden apologized profusely as we helped his parents clean everything back up the best we could.

"I'm so sorry about tonight," his mother said, wrapping me in a hug.

"You have nothing to apologize for," I assured her, and with promises that we will be back soon, without Desmond, we are finally on our way home.

I made Camden sit on the couch in the living room while I ran to get the first aid kit. Seeing him like this broke my heart.

My husband.

For the first time, I allowed myself to imagine that this was real. That we could be together.

He kept trying to brush me off but I insisted that we get him cleaned up. The cut above his eye didn't look too deep, he shouldn't need stitches. So that was good.

"Are you sure you're okay?" I asked for the hundredth time once the last bandage was in place.

"I am, thanks to you," he leaned over and placed a gentle kiss on my cheek.

I decided I had to ask him the burning question on my mind. It had been bothering me most of the night, and all the way home. I had to know the truth. It would consume me if I didn't know. Clearing my throat I asked, "So what you said back there . . . Was it true? Did you really mean it?"

"Which part do you mean?" he asked, raising an eyebrow.

"That I am the only woman you've ever loved?" I held my breath, both wanting, needing to know and also afraid of the answer.

Camden tensed beside me and I immediately regretted asking the question. It was an excruciating few minutes before he finally answered. "Yes," he said, nodding slowly. "It's time. I've been in love with you for a long time now. But," he said before I could say anything, "it's a long story and I promise you, I will tell it to you later, but for now I really need to shower and I'd like to get some sleep."

I nodded, secretly elated. "I understand," I said. Camden stood, kissing me on the top of my head before heading to his room.

I couldn't believe it! Camden Luxmore was in love with me! I have never felt so excited before.

Maybe something really will happen between us after all.

I cleaned up the mess in the living room and skipped off to my bedroom, although I was much too excited to get any sort of sleep tonight. I know I'll have to be careful though. I have to pace myself. Admitting he was in love with me wasn't an easy thing for Camden to do.

I have to give him time, even if that's not what my heart wanted.

Chapter Nineteen

I opened my eyes the next morning, after finally being able to get some sleep, with a huge smile on my face. This is the happiest I've felt in a long time.

Camden and I had been married for a few weeks now. Despite the fight that occurred last night between him and his brother, I felt that we had made significant progress in our relationship.

In the beginning this felt like nothing more than another business deal for Camden. And that I was just a pawn, something for him to use to get himself ahead in the game, in the business.

But now, after last night's admission, something's changed, forever shifted. And the possibility that we could become a real couple has finally presented itself.

And I was determined to make it happen.

Even before the fight I was beginning to see him as more than just my boss. He was a man. A strong, caring, sexy, sensitive man.

He was my husband.

Now if only I could get him to see me as his wife.

I quickly got dressed for work and headed on out to the kitchen for breakfast. Camden was nowhere in sight. Odd, since he was usually up and ready to go before I was. I check the time. Yeah, he should definitely be up by now.

As I walked to his bedroom I noticed the door was still closed. He usually leaves it open a bit when he's not inside. I knock softly, gently calling out his name.

Nothing.

I knock again, louder this time, calling out his name once more.

Again, nothing.

He didn't respond to my texts and calls either, leaving me worried. What if he was more injured than we thought from the fight? Sometimes injuries can present themselves later on. I paced back-and-forth, worried out of my mind. He could be seriously hurt.

I was about to call his doctor or his parents or someone to come and check on him when my phone pinged. It was a message from Camden.

I'm fine. I promise, head on into work alone.

That's all it said. I looked back at his door and bit my bottom lip, still unsure of what I should do. But then again, if he says he's fine, I should just believe him. After all, I had no reason not to.

So I hesitantly made myself a quick breakfast ,and when he still hadn't appeared, decided to head on into work.

An hour goes by and still no sign of Camden. Even though he said he was fine, worry settles in my gut. He's never missed a day of work. It's too important to him. Hell, he's never even been late, not even once in all the years I have worked for him.

Lisa comes around the corner of the office as I'm staring at Camden's office door. "He should be in soon," she says, breaking me out of my fog of worry.

I take the cup of coffee that she offered me, glad for the extra jolt of caffeine. "Huh?"

She nodded her head towards Camden's office. "He called a bit ago saying he had an emergency meeting. There were no details, but then again I didn't think to ask," she shrugged.

He called Lisa and not me? I wasn't informed of any sort of meeting. He never said a word to me about it this morning.

Maybe that's why he had locked himself in his bedroom this morning. Why he had ignored my calls and texts. He was dealing with something important happening with the company. I wonder what was so bad that he had to attend right away and not even inform me. Hopefully we didn't have another Trent situation on our hands.

"Thank you," I said to Lisa, who smiled hesitantly and walked back to her desk. It wasn't unusual for her to get calls instead of me, especially since I did tend to get busy a lot of the time and had to step away from my desk. Lisa is sort of like Camden's secondary secretary.

Still, I didn't like this one bit. It never bothered me before when Lisa was informed of something before I was. Then again it's not very often that our boss gets into a fist fight and ends up injured.

The rest of the workday dragged on slowly, with no sign of Camden. I texted him a few times during the day and they had all gone on unanswered. So I spent the last couple of hours watching the clock ,counting down the minutes until I could go home and check on him in person.

The second the clock struck six I grabbed my purse and ran out of the building.

I didn't know what I expected to find when I got home. Camden's bedroom door was finally open. I peeked inside, calling his name. When there was no answer I pushed the door open further, but his bedroom was empty. So was the living room.

I finally found him sitting at the desk in his home office. He was pouring over documents, typing away. I knocked lightly on the door frame.

Camden's head shot up, startled. He checked his watch and scrubbed his hand over his face. "Oh, I didn't realize it was so late already."

"Is this where you've been hiding out?" I ask, attempting to lighten the mood.

"Not hiding," he said, "but yes. I needed to get some work done, but I also didn't want anyone seeing me like this." The bruises on his face were already beginning to fade. The cut near his eye seemed to be the worst thing. We'd have to get that bandage changed soon. I bet if I played around with his hair I could get the injury covered. But it was unlike him to be worried so much about it. I wondered if something else was going on.

"I was worried about you," I said, my voice a little shaky. I was just so relieved to find out he was okay. "I was afraid something bad might have happened to you. That you were injured worse than I thought."

"Hey," he said, getting up out of his chair. He walked around the desk and wrapped his arms around me and I melted into him. "I'm okay, I promise. I just didn't want anyone at work to see me like this and start asking questions. Besides," he said resting his chin on the top of my head. "Desmond isn't that strong. He barely touched me."

I chuckled, even though I felt like crying. I really have been worried about him all day. I was so scared he really got hurt. I squeezed him a little tighter, never wanting to let him go.

"You're really that worried about me, huh?" he asked. I nodded into his chest. "I'm sorry. Come on, let's go have dinner together."

I changed out of my work clothes and we cooked a simple meal of pasta and salad together. I kept watching him out of the corner of my eye for any signs of an injury, but he seemed perfectly fine. I gave in and enjoyed the meal we made together.

Later on in the evening, after Camden and finished up the work in his office, I found him sitting on the couch in the living room. He had his eyes closed, but I could tell he wasn't sleeping. Just listening to the sounds of the water while he relaxed.

That was one of the things I loved about Camden's house, although I hadn't had time to stop and appreciate it until now. One wall of his living room consisted of floor-to-ceiling windows. Situated right on the other side of the window was the pond with the small fountains in it.

The place we got married.

The living room was filled with the soothing sounds from the water and I could feel my worry from the day begin to melt away. I watched Camden, his chest rising and falling with each breath. Somehow, he looks even sexier when he's relaxing. I couldn't help myself and walked right over to him.

He opened his eyes when he heard me, but I didn't stop. I want him, and I'm done being afraid to show it.

"Anna, what's ..."

I lowered my lips to his, cutting him off. His moans tell me that he doesn't mind one bit. I deepened the kiss as I lifted my leg over him, moving until I was straddling him.

Camden moves his hands between my legs, letting out a gasp when he discovers my surprise. "No panties," he whispers, his voice husky. "Already so wet too."

"Always for you," I answered, molding my lips back to his.

Camden wasted no time in unzipping his pants, letting his erection spring free. With one hand he aligns himself with my slick opening. I sink down on top of him, taking all of him deep inside me. Electricity fills my body at every thrust, every touch. I move up and down, taking him as deeply as I can while his hands roam over every inch of my body.

Camden pulls my top down and takes my hard, sensitive nipples in his mouth. He slowly runs his tongue over them and blows cool air on them, my body filling with so many different sensations.

He grabs my hips, thrusting faster and harder as he brings me to orgasm. I clench around him as he comes deep inside of me.

I lower my forehead to his, panting as I try to catch my breath.

"That was amazing," he said.

"There's plenty more where that came from," I tease.

"In that case," he said, kissing me forcefully. He takes me one more time and then he brings me into his bedroom. There we shower together and have round three right there under the waterfall shower.

"Sleep with me," he whispers, holding my wet naked body as I came down from my orgasm. "Spend the night here, next to me."

I nod eagerly. Spending the night next to my husband sounds like the perfect end to the day .

Chapter Twenty

I had just fallen into a blissful sleep when my phone rang loudly. I cursed myself for not putting it on silent like I normally do. But when I saw the time and Julia's name flash across the screen, I jumped up to answer it.

Julia was frantic on the other end of the line. "We're at the hospital," she began, and my heart stopped. "It's Tyler. He stopped . . . he stopped breathing. He passed out and he wasn't breathing." She broke down in heavy sobs.

The phone slipped from my hands and onto the bed. Camden, seeing the shock up on my face, picked up the phone and talked to Julia in my place.

Before I knew it he had somehow gotten me dressed and in the car, and we were on our way to meet Julia at the hospital. Once there, Cam led the way, speaking to the nurse who pointed us in the right direction.

Julia was pacing back-and-forth in the hallway when we finally found her. I called her name and we ran to each other. I threw my arms around her while she sobbed on my shoulder.

Once she finally calmed down a little I asked her what exactly had happened. She sniffled and Camden went and found her some tissues. "Thank you," she said, accepting them from him. She turned her attention back to me. "It came out of nowhere. Tyler has been acting normal all day. Nothing seemed to be wrong. There were no signs that he was sick or had been feeling bad. We were putting the kids to bed when we heard a scream. So we raced to the boys room to find Jason in tears. Tyler was passed out on the floor." Julia paused to blow her nose and wipe away some of the tears streaming down her face.

"Do they know the cause?" Camden asked, surprising us both. He looked at Julia with concern in his eyes.

"I think so," she replied. "He has irregular heart-beats. Cardiac . . . something."

"Cardiac arrhythmia," Cam finished for her.

Julia nodded. "Yea, that."

My eyes grew wide. "Is it serious?"

Julia shook her head. "They're not sure. They don't think so, but they want to run a few more tests."

Camden straightened up. "Julia, would you mind if I talked to the doctor for a minute?"

She looked at me, uncertainty in her eyes. I just shrugged. "I guess," she said, never taking her eyes off me. Cam gave a quick nod and disappeared down the hall, in search of the doctor."

"What do you think he wants to talk to the doctor about?" Julia asked once he was gone.

"Beats me," I said, shaking my head. "But how are you? How is everyone else?"

"Well, I'm a mess," she confessed. "The kids are understandably shaken up. Mark took them over to his parent's house for a few nights. He should be here any minute now." Her hands trembled in her lap. I reached over and took them in mine.

"Hey," I said as soothingly as I could. "It's okay. Tyler will be okay. We will all get through this together."

She shook her head sadly. "I don't know, Anna. The tests he needs are so expensive, and if he does end up needing surgery I . . ."

"Don't need to worry," Cam said, reappearing at my side. "All of his bills are paid for and any future test or procedures will be paid for as well. You don't have to worry about a single thing."

Julia's eyes grew wide. "What?"

He put his hand up. "We're family now. Family takes care of one another. They're moving Tyler to a different room as we speak."

Mark showed up right after and was filled in on everything. He burst into tears, throwing himself onto Camden, who hugged him awkwardly. I don't think I've ever seen Mark cry. He was just so grateful to be able to have his son receive the best care possible.

The room Tyler was moved into looked similar to a large suite at a hotel, except filled and stocked with medical equipment. Cam ordered every test that Tyler could possibly need and told them not to worry about cost or anything.

While Julia and Mark were fussing over Tyler, I walked over to Cam and grabbed his hand. "Thank you for this," I whispered. "You really didn't have to do this, but I also really appreciate it. You have no idea how much I appreciate it."

"Of course," he said, leaning over to give me a quick kiss. "Anything for you." My heart swelled just looking at the man. I don't know what I did to deserve him.

We stayed most of the day at the hospital as the

doctors ran some of their tests. They said that although it wasn't that serious right now, the possibility of surgery was still high.

We could tell they wanted to be alone with their son, so Camden signed the authorization of payment for any procedure needed and we quietly left the hospital. Before leaving I gave Julia one more hug and promised to visit her later.

We went home for a quick nap and then to the office to at least get in a couple hours of work.

Chapter Twenty-One

The next few days flew by in a blur. Tyler had a few more tests done, where it was determined that he would, in fact, be needing surgery. It wasn't life-threatening, so the actual surgery was scheduled for another two days. I was constantly checking my phone for any update from Julia.

"He's going to be fine." I jumped at the sound of Cam's voice. My phone flew out of my hands and landed on his feet. He raised an eyebrow at me as he bent over to retrieve it off the floor for me.

"I'm sorry," I said quickly. My cheeks burned with embarrassment. I know better than to have my phone on at work. Being caught by the boss of all people made it so much worse.

"It's fine," he waved me off, handing me back my

phone. I snuck one last look at it before setting it down on my desk. "But you better get ready. We have a meeting in about twenty minutes."

A meeting? How could I have forgotten? I've been so focused on Tyler that it must've completely slipped my mind. Feeling flustered, I began quickly rummaging through the stacks of papers on my desk trying hard to remember which meeting it was and what it was all about.

Camden put his hand down on the papers in my hand. "It's okay. All you need is your purse and something to take notes with. I have everything else," he said, holding up his briefcase.

I blew out a quick sigh of relief, grabbing my purse and a notebook and following closely behind him. I can't believe I'm acting this way. I'm usually so on top of things at work. I followed him silently to the car, promising myself that I would get it together and start focusing more. Starting with this meeting.

I followed Cam into a new restaurant that had just opened up. I remember hearing about this place, but I've never been. Luxmore Inc was acquiring shops and restaurants all the time, so I figured today must be a discussion about a possible partnership.

I really wished I had remembered so I could have prepared better. I felt so ashamed. I didn't know anyone's names, or anything at all about this restaurant or the dishes they served.

"Right this way, Mr. Luxmore," a host greets us, opening the doors to a private room. Camden nodded and thanked him, and we went inside.

There were candles and roses everywhere, and the lights had been dimmed. This was an odd setting for a meeting. Perhaps the owner was wanting to impress Camden. People did tend to go all out when vying for Camden's attention. Everyone wanted to be a part of Luxmore Inc. You carry their name, you carry success.

He walked over to the table, pulling out a chair for me. Thanking him, I sat down and began to get my note taking supplies ready and situated. I was determined to pay attention and not screw this up.

"You won't be needing those," Camden said as he took my notebook away.

"I . . ."

Camden just smiled, a playful twinkle dancing in his eyes.

"Then why did you tell me there was a meeting and had me bring those?"

He sat back in his chair, folding his arms over his chest. "How else was I supposed to sneak you out of the office for a date?"

Oh.

I look around. The candles and roses weren't to impress Camden. They were for me.

I felt like an idiot for not noticing.

Camden leaned forward, taking my hand in his. "It's been such a hectic week. I figured you could use a little time to just sit and relax. And a little alone time with me," he added with a wink.

This man was so damn thoughtful. I got up out of my chair and walked around the table, sliding into his lap. "Thank you Camden. For everything. For caring about my sister, and helping Tyler, and this," I gesture around the room. "You don't know how much I appreciate it. How much I appreciate you."

"You can thank me properly later on," he said, bringing my mouth down to his.

We were interrupted a few seconds later as the waiter cleared his throat. Sheepishly I slid off of Camden's lap and quickly sat down in my seat, avoiding eye contact with the waiter. I could see Cam's shoulders shaking a little with his laughter. I didn't think it was very funny. I was mortified.

"Your wine," he says, presenting the bottle to Camden. He gives him an approving nod and then our glasses are filled up. I quickly drained mine as soon as we were alone.

"I can't believe we almost got caught," I said in a

loud whisper.

"Why? We weren't doing anything," Cam said, wiggling his eyebrows. "Yet."

"I was sitting on your lap," I hissed.

Cam got a devilish look in his eyes. "I know," he growled. It's one of my favorite places for you to be."

The waiter chose that moment to bring us our food that Camden had pre-ordered for us. My face and the back of my neck were on fire. I'm pretty sure I'll never be able to show my face in this restaurant again.

The rest of lunch went by uneventfully, thankfully. I never knew how much I needed this, to just sit here and have a quiet lunch with my husband.

By the time we were done eating, I felt almost completely back to normal. I checked my messages only once before putting my phone away, promising myself not to touch it for at least another hour or two.

"You know," Cam whispered, that devilish look back in his eyes, "if you really want to you can meet me in my office. So you can properly thank me for today."

Shivers ran up the length of my entire body. It didn't take much for this man to turn me on. "Right behind you," I whispered back.

"I'll need to see those notes from today's meeting," Cam said loudly once we were near his office. Terry and Lisa looked up upon hearing his voice.

"I'll be right on it," I said, giving my coworkers a little wave. I hate lying to them. I would love nothing more than to open up and tell them I'm dating Camden.

It may not be real at the moment, but I had a feeling it was heading that way.

I set my purse down on my desk and pulled out the notebook that I had originally brought along to take notes with, to bring with me into Camden's office. I hurried up and followed behind him.

I nearly bumped into him as he had been standing just inside the office door. "Camden, what . . ." I began to ask, but his eyes flashed with anger. I followed his gaze to his desk where Desmond was seated. He was in Camden's seat, and had his feet up on the desk, his hands clasped behind his head, looking relaxed. He was trying his hardest to look every bit of the CEO that he wasn't, or ever would be.

"What the hell do you think you're doing here?" Cam demanded.

"Relax." Desmond said, standing up out of the office chair. "I'm not here to cause any trouble. Besides," he scanned his eyes over the office, "someday this will all be mine. As it rightfully is. You're just keeping the seat warm for me." He laughed as Camden clenched his fists.

"You need to get the hell out of here," he said. You could feel the anger coming off Camden in waves.

Desmond put his hands up in the air, as if in defeat. "All right, all right. I'm out. But I will be back to take what's mine," he warned. He opened the door and just before exiting the office, turned to address both me and his brother. "I forgot the real reason I came here today. I'm hosting a party at mom and dad's house this weekend. You two better be there. You wouldn't want to disappoint mom and dad." He laughed again, throwing me a wink before finally leaving.

I finally let out the breath I have been holding. It's always so stressful whenever Desmond is around. Why did that man have to always be so infuriating?

Cam walked right up to his desk, grabbing the party invite Desmond had left. He ripped it up into tiny little pieces, letting it fall into the trashcan like evil confetti.

"We're going, aren't we?" I asked, already knowing the answer.

"Yes," he sighed heavily. Camden sank down in his chair, taking his head in his hands. I hated seeing him like this, especially after the perfect lunch we just had.

Leave it to Desmond to spoil the mood.

Camden looked up at me. "Come here," he said

softly. I set my notebook on the couch and walked over to him. I stood in between his legs, putting my arms around his shoulders and pulling him into a hug. Camden sighed against my stomach. I hate the effect his brother has on him. How he's always fighting him for what isn't his.

After a minute or so of holding onto each other, Camden pulled back a little and looked up at me. I recognized that look in his eyes.

"You know," he said, "this desk has now been left with the tainted memory of my brother. How about you and I remedy that?"

He wrapped both hands around my waist, effortlessly lifting me up on top of his desk. I gasped as he lifted both my legs over my shoulders while pulling me closer to him. He looked into my eyes and I could see the want, the need in them that mirrored my own. He leaned in and kissed me hard, for about five seconds before moving down between my legs. He glides his fingers over the fabric of my lace thong.

"Already wet," he murmurs, raising an eyebrow. It's amazing what this man does to me.

I placed my palms on either side of myself on the desk, closing my eyes as he slid the fabric to the side. I bit my bottom lip to stop the moan from escaping as his tongue slowly brushed over my opening.

"You're mine, Anna. Don't ever forget that."

I shook my head but before I could answer him, Camden flicked his tongue in a steady rhythm over my already swollen clit. I thread my hands through his hair, trying my hardest not to scream, even though it's all I want to do.

"Camden," I begged breathlessly. He stopped and looked up at me, pure lust in his eyes. "I need you," I whispered impatiently.

He lowered my legs back down to his desk, stepping back just enough to unzip and lower his pants before pulling me to the edge of his desk. I was wet and more than ready for him, and he slid easily inside me, filling up every inch. With one arm wrapped around me and the other steadying himself, he thrusted hard and fast. As though he can't get enough of me. It might also have something to do with the fact that someone could walk in on us at any second. Cam forgot to close the blinds, but right now I couldn't care about that. All I wanted was Cam.

It's not long before we're both close. "Anna!" He called out my name, and I clenched around him, riding the waves of my orgasm. Cam convulsed against me, leaning down to place his forehead against mine, his breath ragged.

"Do you see what you do to me?" he whispered.

"How am I supposed to get any work done with my sexy wife working just outside my office door?"

"You'll have to figure it out," I laughed, sliding off the desk to clean myself up and fix my clothes. "We're supposed to be a secret."

"But for how long?" Cam asked, tightening his belt. "How much longer do I have to keep it hidden from the world that I'm married and in love with the greatest woman alive?"

In love?

"I . . . I . . ." I stammered, not knowing what to say. Was Camden Luxmore truly in love with me? He couldn't possibly be. This was all supposed to be fake, just temporary. Now he wanted to tell everyone that we're together? And that we're married? Telling people at the office could be bad news for me. Starting up rumors of unfair treatment and all that.

But what if it could be true, even a little bit?

Could I ever be a woman worthy of Camden's love?

"We can talk about this later," I said, planting a kiss on his lips. I returned to work unsure of how I was supposed to get anything done after that.

Camden's confession confused the hell out of me.

Chapter Twenty-Two

The day of Desmond's big party has arrived. He's been calling and texting Camden every day to remind him of it. I don't get what was so important about this party. The Luxmore's held several of them throughout the year. No one's ever made this much of a fuss before.

Then again the rest of the Luxmore family was all well liked and respected. I suppose it does make sense that he would have to put in a little more effort just to get anyone to attend his party.

Camden had to meet with his father about something pertaining to the company, so I took the opportunity to go for a walk.

I rested my arms against the railing as I stared out

over the river. I took in a deep cleansing breath. It's been so long since I've been able to do this. I have lived near the water all my life, and used to come down to the boardwalk daily. Being on or around water was my happy place.

But once I began working for Luxmore Inc, all my free time seemed to have evaporated. Because of Camden's passion and drive for the business, he could be somewhat demanding, especially of your time. At first I resented him for it, but then I came to realize he didn't act that way just because he wanted to be an ass.

Although, he was good at that.

He did it because he wanted the company to succeed. *He* wanted to succeed.

And I've grown to admire that about him.

It's truly amazing how much your life can change and how fast. Everything that's happened to me in the past few months alone makes my head spin.

I stopped to think about it. I never imagined that one day I would be working for one of the most powerful and influential CEOs of our time. I certainly never imagined myself married to him. There was only one time in my life where I thought that maybe I'd like to get married someday.

"Anna?"

Startled, I turned my head in the direction of the voice. There, standing a few feet away from me, was the reason I ever thought about marriage in the first place.

Jackson Greer. We had dated back in college and had quickly become very serious. He was the only man I had ever thought about possibly marrying. But as it turned out, I was the only one that felt that way. The minute I so much as hinted at the fact that I may be wanting to get married, Jackson took off. Leaving the state and taking my heart along with him.

This was a couple years before I began working at Luxmore Inc. I'm sure this in part contributed to the fact that I haven't dated in a really long time.

I hadn't thought about my ex in years and now here he was, standing right in front of me.

"Jackson?" I asked, not being able to hide my surprise. "How are you? How have you been?"

"I've been pretty good," he tells me, coming in to give me a quick, awkward hug.

Jackson let go of me and stood back a couple of steps. "You look amazing," he stated, roaming his eyes over me.

I faked a smile, but didn't say anything in response. Jackson shoved his hands into the front pockets of his jeans as he rocked back-and-forth on his heels.

This was awkward. He was awkward. And I hated that he was here, more than I hated having to attend Desmond's party tonight. How dare he come in and ruin the only peaceful moment I've had in months.

"I guess there's still a lot I need to apologize for," he said, breaking the silence between us. "I can see it in your eyes."

I looked away from him and back out on the river. "I don't need an apology," I told him, which was the truth. I wanted nothing at all from this man anymore.

Jackson took a step closer to me, but stopped once he saw how tense I was. He looked away from me and down at his feet, taking in a deep breath and letting it out forcefully. "I guess I deserved that. I was kind of an ass when we dated."

Kind of? The man completely shattered my heart, as well as my views of relationships in general. Yet he had no idea. But I wasn't about to explain that to him. I wouldn't give him the satisfaction of knowing just how much he had affected me in the past.

"I was scared," he continued, even though I never said a word. "Once you mentioned marriage I freaked out. We were young, and you were my first real girl-friend. I didn't have much experience and I didn't want to be tied down to just one girl. I wanted to get out and explore, have some fun and freedom, without any consequences."

Each word he said was like a knife in my heart, chipping off another piece. How could he stand here saying these things to me, thinking they'll make me feel better?

"As soon as my grandfather offered me a position at his company, I knew I had to take it." He paused to look up at me, and I could see a flash of hurt in his eyes. "But just a few months after I accepted it, I realized what a mistake I had made. But by then I figured it was too late. I was sure you had moved on."

I didn't know what to say. I had no words for this man. I didn't want to make him feel better. He didn't deserve it.

"Do you ever think about me?" He asked. I shook my head honestly.

Jackson let out a pained sigh, looking away from me. "I guess I deserve that too. But I miss you, Anna. It took losing you to realize it. I can't stop thinking about you, even after all these years. What do you think about us . . ."

"She already has a man," came a voice from behind me. I've never been so relieved to see Camden in my life. He walked right up behind me, placing his arms around me and kissing the top of my head. "Sorry I'm late, babe. Things took longer than I thought at the office."

I leaned back until my head rested against his chest. "It's okay," I whispered. "You're here now."

Jackson just stared, his eyes wide. "I'm sorry," he said. "I didn't know she had a boyfriend."

"Husband." Cam corrected him. He took a business card out of his wallet and handed it over. "Mrs. Luxmore likes to keep it a secret. While I, on the other hand, I want to shout it to the world that we're in love." Cam gave me a squeeze and I squeezed him right back.

My heart was pounding though at the thought that he had just called me Mrs. Luxmore. It sounded strange, but I secretly loved it. He referred to me as his wife in private, but never out in public. I wanted to hear it again and again.

Jackson just looked at Camden, his eyes wide with recognition. Then he looked at me and his expression changed to one of deceit. Clearing his throat, he stuck out his hand. "Jackson Greer," he said to Cam. "An old friend of Anna's."

Cam shook his hand, with a little more force than he probably should have. "Camden Luxmore, *husband* of Anna."

I tried not to laugh at Cam's blatant display of jealousy and possessiveness. I've never seen this side of him before and I have got to say, I don't hate it.

Jackson put his hands back into his front pockets. "I guess I should be going," he said. I nodded.

"Us, too," Cam said, checking his watch. "We have an important family function to get to. It was nice meeting you, Jason."

"Jackson," he corrected him, his face scrunching up.

Cam waved him away. "Whatever. Let's go babe," he said, turning us both to leave. I didn't look back to make sure that Jackson walked away. I just laughed and poked Cam in the side.

"You're funny when you're jealous," I teased him.

Cam let go of me, straightening his suit jacket. "I don't know what you're talking about. Camden Luxmore does not get jealous," he said, sticking his chin up in the air.

"Sure, whatever you say *babe*," I said, laughing harder. I spotted Camden's car and took off running, with Camden chasing after me. He caught up to me just as we reached the car. He placed his hands on either side of me on the car, boxing me in.

"Promise me you'll stay away from him," he said, pointing down the boardwalk.

I wrapped my arms around him. "You're the only

one for me, I promise," I told him, standing on my toes to kiss him. The possessiveness I saw in his eyes was somehow a huge turn on. I reached up, threading my hands through his hair as I deepened the kiss. He had me pinned up against the car.

If only we didn't have to attend that party . . .

Chapter Twenty-Three

Walking into the Luxmore's backyard, I had a sense of dread washing over me. I leaned into Cam. "Are you sure you're going to be okay?" I asked, referring to the last time the Luxmore brothers had gotten together here. I really hoped tonight we would be able to avoid another bloodbath.

"I'm fine," Cam assured me, bringing his lips to mine. He placed his hand on the small of my back as we descended the stairs to join the rest of his family.

We made one round of the room, greeting everybody. The only person I hadn't seen yet was Desmond. The bastard didn't even show up to his own damn party.

There were tables scattered around the yard that were tastefully decorated. After a few minutes of mingling we were all told to find one and take a seat. Champagne was passed around and we were told not to take a sip yet, as they were to be saved for the toast. Cam and I just looked at each other and shrugged. It seemed no one knew what was going on.

Before I could ask anyone, two figures appeared at the top of the steps underneath a shower of confetti. When it cleared I could see that one of the figures was Desmond. And on his arm . . . was Monica.

He sure knows how to make an entrance, I'll give him that.

Hand in hand Desmond and Monica descended the stairs together. She had a huge smile plastered on her face as she scanned the crowd, seemingly pleased with the turnout. Desmond, on the other hand, never took his eyes off of her. He smiled sweetly at her as they made their way down to us.

They stopped at the bottom of the stairs and were handed a flute of champagne each. All eyes were on the two of them.

"First of all, I would like to thank everyone for being here. It means so much to me. To us," Desmond said, looking over at Monica. "Well, we really don't want to drag this out, because we are just so excited for tonight. You are all here to celebrate our engagement! I proposed to the sexy woman," he said, referring to

Monica, "and she said yes!" He raised his glass and took a sip. Then he pulled Monica in for a sloppy kiss.

There were stunned gasps all around. It seems no one was expecting this news. Slowly, people began to raise their glasses. Then a few began to clap and yell excitedly.

"Well," said Camden, tipping back his entire glass of champagne. "This night just got interesting."

I couldn't agree more. "Do you really think they're in love?" I asked. "I didn't even know they were dating."

"They're in love with power." Camden answered, offering nothing further. Which was true. I don't think it was possible for Desmond to love someone as much as he loved power and money.

At least this should keep her away from Cam, I thought selfishly to myself.

More alcohol was brought out and dance music turned on. Everyone began drinking and headed out to the makeshift dance floor in the garden.

I wasn't quite drunk enough to attempt to dance so I stayed seated while Cam went over to congratulate Desmond along with his parents. He was only gone about five minutes when Monica decided to come over and plopped herself down in the chair next to me. "Enjoying my party?" she asked.

I really didn't want to speak to her, but I nodded, smiling politely. "Congratulations by the way. You must be so happy."

"I am," she said, turning her large diamond ring around on her finger, admiring the way it sparkled in the light.

"This is just the start," she said, suddenly leaning in a little too close for my comfort. "Once Des and I are married, he and I will be taking back everything that is rightfully his. Everything that his brother stole. So you tell Cam to enjoy it while he can. Because the second we're married, we're throwing him out of there. It'll be me and Desmond running the company. The way it should be."

Out of the corner of my eye I could see Cam walking back this way. Monica quickly straightened up. "Watch your back," she warned before hopping out of the chair and disappearing off into the crowd.

"What did she say to you?" Cam asked as he reclaimed his seat. He had a worried and annoyed look in his eyes.

"She told me to watch my back."

"Did she now?" He looks after her, narrowing his eyes. Cam stood up, offering me his hand. "Tell me what else she said over a dance, wifey."

I swear my heart's going to burst every time he

refers to me as his wife. I took his hand and he led me to the dance floor. With one hand on my back, he pulled me in close, so that our bodies were flush together. "Now, talk to me," he whispered as we swayed to the slow song that was playing.

I would rather just dance with Cam, feeling our bodies move together, but I told him everything that Monica said about them wanting to take over the company.

Cam threw his head back and laughed. "Do you want to know a secret?"

I nodded eagerly.

Cam bent down close so he could whisper, his lips brushing over my ears, causing shivers to run through my body.

"Desmond isn't getting anything. He was cut out of the will years ago."

My eyes widened with shock. "Seriously? And he has no idea?"

Cam shook his head. "Not a clue. So they can try all they want, but because of his partying and excessive drug use he's been cut off. He gets nothing of the family company or fortune. He gets the last name and that's it. None of the privileges that come with it."

I tried, but failed to cover my laughter. Serves him right after the way he treated Cam all these years.

"So we'll just let them have their fun," Cam said. "And later on tonight, you and I will have a little fun of our own," he added with a seductive smile. My thighs clenched at that. All of a sudden I couldn't wait to get home.

Chapter Twenty-Four

Every day since Desmond's engagement announcement there had been news articles printed about it. Some were just announcing the happy couples' news while others hinted that maybe there would soon be a change in command at Luxmore Inc.

Desmond and Monica were wasting no time in planting stories and holding interviews and photo shoot after photo shoot. I hated seeing both of their faces splashed all over the news and internet daily.

But I also couldn't wait for their downfall. They had absolutely no idea what's in store for them. I almost wished I could be there when they found out that they would be receiving absolutely nothing. I'd love to see the looks on their faces.

Lisa was sitting and gossiping with me over the

articles when my cell phone rang. I had forgotten to shut it off again. When I picked it up to shut it off I paused at the name flashing across the screen. I held it up to Lisa. Cam's mother was calling me. She never called me, like ever. Dread settled in my stomach.

"Answer it," Lisa said in a whisper.

I cleared my throat. "Hello, Mrs. Luxmore. What can I do for you?" I asked, trying to sound as professional as possible.

She sounded panicked on the other line. "I can't get a hold of Cam. Where is Cam?" she cried.

I looked over at Lisa who just shrugged. "He's around the building somewhere. Can I take a message and have him call you back when I see him?"

"No!" she practically screamed. "When she told me the reason for her call, my heart shattered and I dropped my cell."

Lisa picked it up for me and told Mrs. Luxmore who she was and that I had dropped my phone. Lisa went white as she listened to Mrs Luxmore. She hung up the phone and grabbed my hand, pulling me up out of my seat. "Come on," she said through the tears streaming down her face. "We have got to find Mr. Luxmore. Now."

The two of us ran through the building . It took us about ten minutes to locate Camden, who was just coming out of the boardroom. When he spotted us he walked over, concern filling his eyes. Lisa took a step back, trying and failing to cover her sobs, leaving me to do the dirty work.

"What is it?" he demanded, looking from me to Lisa and back again. "What's wrong?"

"Camden," I cried. "Your mother just called. Your . . . your father has passed. I'm so sorry."

Camden stared straight ahead for a minute before suddenly turning to run out of the building. I couldn't keep up, he was running so fast. I knew where he was headed so I hopped in my car, following not that far behind.

I dialed Lisa's number from the road. "Lis, I'm on my way to the Luxmore mansion with Cam. We most likely won't be back today. Can you please let everyone know?" I sniffled.

"Absolutely," she said in between sobs. "Please be careful."

"I will," I said, hanging up.

I pulled up to the front of the Luxmore mansion and parked next to Camden. He was still sitting in his car in the driver's seat, staring up at the house. My heart ached for him.

I put my car in park and got out, climbing into the passenger side of Cam's car. He looked over at me and

I grabbed his hand. Camden broke down in sobs and leaned into me. I couldn't put my arms around him in this position, so I just held his hands for comfort as he cried on my shoulder.

Once his tears were gone we sat in silence for a few more minutes. I sucked in a deep breath, turning towards him. His eyes were red and swollen, and he just looked lost.

My heart broke.

"You should head in," I said as gently as I could. "I know it's hard but your mother needs you right now."

He nodded. "But what about you?"

I shook my head. "Your family needs you. You all need each other. I'll be waiting at home for you."

Camden sighed, then leaned over and kissed me. It was a kiss full of desperation and sadness, of hope and need. He rested his forehead against mine.

"I'll be waiting, I promise," I whispered.

He gave me one more kiss, then we both exited the car. Before I left I pulled him into a hug, holding him tightly.

"I'm sorry," I whispered. I waited until he was inside the mansion before making the drive back to our house. I cried the entire way. This was all just so sudden. I couldn't imagine the pain Camden was feeling right now.

I walked into the house and something just felt different. I couldn't put my finger on it, but something just fell off. I slowly looked around, checking every room.

Then I noticed it.

In the living room on the table, was a bouquet of flowers and a letter. I wondered who had dropped them off. And more importantly, how they got in here. I noticed the letter was addressed to me. I quickly looked around the room, as if the sender might still be here, watching me from a distance. I was officially creeped out now.

I hesitated for a second before picking it up and opening the letter. It was from Camden's father. My heart began to pound as I read the letter.

My dearest Anna,

If you are reading this, it means I have finally passed on. I had a few things to tell you, but as you know I am a man of very few words. So this will be short and sweet and to the point.

I have known for some time now that I didn't have much time left in this world. I couldn't bring myself to tell my boys, which was the hardest thing I've ever had to do. Perhaps it was selfish of me, but I just couldn't have our last moments together be ones filled with sadness. I needed to see their smiles in my last moments on this earth.

Knowing that my days were numbered, I knew I had to act fast. That's why I had been so adamant that Camden marry as quickly as he did. I can rest in peace now, knowing that he and in turn, the company, will be well taken care of.

I have known for years that Camden was in love with you. Any fool could see it. So you can imagine my happiness at the two of you getting married.

Take care of him. You and I both know just how stubborn that man can get. Take good care of him, look after each other. Don't be afraid of love, it's what makes life worth living.

I can rest well knowing that my company is in capable hands, and that my favorite son (don't tell Desmond) is finally with the woman he loves.

Take care of each other,

All my love,

Walter Luxmore

. . .

I FELL TO MY KNEES, clutching the letter to my chest. He had known that he was going to die. That Camden loved me. He secretly planned out everything, the rest of his life, the future of his company. But most of all, he loved his sons so much. So much that he spent his last days securing their future, as well as their happiness.

Walter Luxmore was not the monster he presented himself to be while running Luxmore Inc. He was just a father, who wanted nothing but the best for his family.

Camden came home hours later, looking worse than when I had left him. I showed him the letter and we both broke down, holding each other as we fell asleep in each other's arms.

Chapter Twenty-Five

The week following Walters' death had been tough. It's been a struggle getting Cam to eat or drink anything. And sleep had been proven impossible. When he was in bed he tossed and turned all night. I hated not being able to do anything to comfort him. It broke my heart seeing my husband so broken.

As I stood in front of the mirror getting ready for the day, I glanced over at Cam as he was getting ready himself. He just goes through the motions while his head is off somewhere completely different. It pained me to see him like this.

"Will you be in the office today?" I ask him gently. Lately he's been working mostly out of the office. I assumed because it held so many memories of his father. It had been Walter's office before Cam took it over.

"I may stop by later in the evening," he said, not bothering to look at me as he finished buttoning up his shirt. "I have a new project going on that I must oversee first."

I nod silently. He's had so many new projects since his father's death. But he never offered any details about any of them. I didn't push the subject either though. I knew Cam needed some space during this trying time.

He turned to leave and I walked over to him, wrapping my arms around his waist. He looked surprised at first but then he wrapped his own arms around me as well. Leaning my head against his chest I asked him, "You know I'm always here for you, right?"

"I do." He pressed a kiss to the top of my head. "I wouldn't have been able to get through this time without you. Thank you," he whispered.

I stood up on my toes until my lips met his. I've missed him. Even little touches like this I have missed dearly. Cam kissed me back, leaving me full of need, but he broke apart from our kiss, telling me he needed to go so that he's not late.

I sighed, grabbing my purse to head into work. It's

days like these though, where I get a glimpse of the old Camden. I can't wait for him to come back to me.

I had only been at work for two hours when Julia called. "Cam's at my house," she said before I even had a chance to say hello.

"He's what?" I asked, thoroughly confused .

"Camden is at my house. He's been here all morning. You should get down here. I'll explain when you get here."

I hung up the phone and walked to Lisa's office. "I have to head out," I explained. "Something with Camden." Her, John, and Terry all nodded in understanding. Everyone could see that he'd been a little off lately. They all knew the reason, too. I smiled tightly at my coworkers and turned to leave, promising to return soon.

I don't know what I was expecting when I pulled up at Julia's, but it certainly wasn't this. There were construction trucks and crews. Pick up trucks and tools, everywhere. It was utter chaos. I fought my way through the mass of people and into the house. "What is all this?" I asked Julia once I finally located her. She was upstairs in one of her kids' rooms, throwing clothes into a suitcase.

Julia looked up at me, a wary expression on her face. "Ask your man," she said, pointing to Camden.

He was standing in the middle of the hall talking to a man about something intensely. Both were wearing hardhats and I can't help but think how sexy he looked in it. Especially with the sleeves of his shirt rolled up past his elbows.

I walked over to Camden as the man he was talking to nodded and turned away, walking down the stairs. "Hi," I said, a confused look on my face. "What's going on here?"

"Renovating," he said, pouring over the plans in his hands.

"Renovating?" I asked. I was going to need more than that.

He stopped and looked up at me for the first time. "Tyler's been home from his surgery, but he's going to need long-term care," he stated, a concerned look filling his eyes. "Your sister and her family live in such a small place, there's no room for the equipment he'll need," he said as he walked into the room where Julia was still packing.

I followed him in, still slightly confused. "So what exactly are you doing?"

"He's making us go away," Jason said stubbornly.

Cam turned to look at him. "I'm not making you go away," he corrected. "I'm sending you to a hotel for a little bit while the construction is taking place. That's all. You'll like it, I promise."

I couldn't believe what I was hearing. Had he consulted Julia about this? Were she and Mark okay with just uprooting their kids, even for a little bit? Julia just shrugged when I looked at her.

Cam turned his attention back to me. "Don't worry," he said, placing his hands on my shoulders. "They're going to be very well taken care of. I'm seeing to it personally. I'm putting them up in the best hotel money can buy. They'll have everything they'll ever need. And, with the amount of people I've hired we'll have them back in their new and improved home before you know it.

I didn't know what to say. I thought all this time he was out making deals with businesses, not renovating my sister's house. My heart swelled with pride. He couldn't have saved his father, so now he's doing everything he could to save Tyler."

Camden Luxmore truly was amazing.

There was still a ton of work to do so I volunteered to help get Julia, Mark, and the kids all packed and settled into their temporary home.

The suite Cam had rented for them was larger and nicer than any hotel room I've ever stayed in. It was even nicer than my last house.

Once all of their belongings had been brought up and the kids were occupied with TV and some food, Julia and I snuck out to the balcony.

"So," I said, taking a seat next to her. The view of the city was breathtaking. "How are you, really?"

Julia sighed heavily, sinking down into the chair. "Honestly, I have no idea," she laughed. Camden came to me a few days ago with the idea, but I didn't take him seriously. I mean, how could I? Never in my wildest dreams did I ever think that anyone would do something like this for us. It's . . ."

"Too much?" I offered.

She nodded. "Yes. But you don't know how much I appreciate it. I've never been able to give the kids the life they deserved. We've always been just barely scraping by. They never once complained about having to share a room, but I just know they all secretly wished they had their own private space. I just feel guilty that I'm not the one to be able to provide them with it."

Julia sniffled, wiping away the tears that had escaped and were trailing down her face. I reached over, taking her hand in mine. "Hey," I said in a soothing voice. "I know you've always done all you could for your family. You are a wonderful mother. Never doubt yourself. Life is never fair," I tell her.

Which is true, she's the best mom I know. I'm not just saying that because she's my sister. I truly meant it.

She patted my hand. "I know," she said. "It's just hard sometimes. "Ah," she said, letting out a huge breath. "You are so lucky that you have someone who loves you as much as Cam does."

I snapped my head in her direction. "You heard me," she laughed. Then she straightened up in her seat, a serious expression taking over her face.

"I'm sorry," she began. "I know I've doubted Cam and his intentions from the start. I thought that whatever was going on between the two of you wasn't anything serious, just a fling. And I'm sorry. I'm so sorry that I said some horrible and nasty things. And I'm sorry I missed out on your wedding. I'm so sorry I haven't been the sister that you need," she cried.

She looked into my eyes and I could see just how much she meant it. How much she regretted her past actions. I pulled her into a hug, fighting off tears of my own. "It's okay, I promise. I probably would've acted the same way in your position."

She pulled away, staring out over the city. "He really does love you, you know," she said it as more of a statement.

I nodded, not really fully believing it. As much as I wanted to, I was scared to hope.

Julia sensed my unease. "Don't let your insecurities get in your way," she said. "That man is truly head over heels for you. Why else would he pay for a complete renovation of your sister's house?"she asked, her eyebrows raised in question.

I just sat back and laughed, wondering if it was true. This was a huge thing he was doing for my sister and her family. He wouldn't be going through with all of this if he didn't have feelings for me, right?

Against my better judgment, hope filled my heart.

IMPRESSIVELY, Julia's house was completed in just over three weeks. I honestly have no idea how Cam managed to make that happen.

At first her kids were reluctant to leave the hotel, where they had been completely pampered and spoiled. But their tune changed as soon as they stepped inside their new home.

It must've been at least three times the size it originally was. Each of the kids had their own spacious room, complete with their own private bathroom.

Tyler's room was equipped with everything he could possibly need medically. Cam also told them that if needed, he would also hire a private at-home nurse.

Julia and Mark were so grateful that they both

thanked him nonstop as they toured the new home. I followed along silently, fighting back tears of my own. This man was truly a blessing.

"Thank you," I whispered as Julia and Mark checked out their new master suite complete with hot tub. I have to admit I was jealous of that feature.

Cam turned to kiss me on the forehead. "I told you, now that we are married I would take care of both you and your family. No need to thank me."

For the first time since Walter's death, Camden smiled. Really smiled. It warmed my heart to see him like this.

Julia offered to make dinner for Camden as a small thank you. She was so excited to use the new fully equipped kitchen. It was impressive, looking almost as if it belonged in a fancy restaurant instead of a home.

Cam took her up on that offer, and we all spent the evening together, just one big happy family.

Chapter Twenty-Six

The next morning I woke up to the smell of coffee and bacon. I looked over to Cam's side of the bed to find it empty. I quickly got dressed and walked out of the kitchen.

I was greeted to the sight of Cam cooking us breakfast. He was wearing only a smile and his pajama pants, which hung low on his hips. Oh, how I have missed this sight.

Admittedly, it was his smile that I missed the most.

"Good morning," he beamed, spotting me. He abandoned what he was doing and walked over, grabbing me by the waist and lifting me up on the counter. He stood in between my legs, placing his palms on either side of me on the counter.

"Well, good morning to you too," I laughed.

He grabbed the back of my head, pulling me in for a long, passionate kiss. One that left me breathless.

"What was that for?" I asked, playfully hooking my hands behind his head.

"I just missed you," he said with a smile.

We were both startled by the toaster popping. "I suppose I should go finish breakfast," he laughed, and I slid off the counter.

He had made a full spread this morning. I haven't eaten this good in forever. The past few weeks I've just managed to just grab a bagel on my way out the door.

We ate breakfast, talking and laughing like we used to. I had really missed this. It seemed as if Camden was well on his way to be coming his old self again.

We even went into the office together, having a full productive day. Cam managed to snag some big time clients, and I got caught up on everything that I had been slacking on over the past few weeks. I vowed never again to let myself get this way at work again.

Before we knew it was time to clock out and head home.

The second we got in the door I set my purse on the table and Camden scooped me up in his arms, carrying me to the bedroom.

He set me on the bed, stepping back to loosen his tie. He slid it off, dropping it to the floor. The bed dipped a little with his weight as he crawled in and hovered over me. I saw so many emotions flash in his eyes. "I'm so sorry I've been distant," he said, his eyes falling to my lips. "I've missed you so much."

"I missed you too," I said in a whisper, reaching up to meet his lips. Cam kissed me with built up passion and need. Everything he'd been neglecting to let himself feel over the past few weeks.

We ripped each other's clothes off, tossing them to the floor. Cam didn't hesitate, lining himself up with my entrance and slamming into me, giving me what I needed.

He increased his pace, thrusting hard and fast.

"Cam, I . . ." I panted. He looked at me, his gaze heated. I could feel myself already about to come. "Cam!" I screamed out as my muscles clenched around his cock. The intensity of the orgasm was almost too much for me. Wave after wave of pleasure washed over me and we soon collapsed on the bed, holding each other as we tried to catch our breath.

I have missed this so much. Not only the mind blowing sex, but just Cam, here in my arms.

We held each other for a while, until Cam rolled over on his side. He propped himself up on his elbow to look at me. "You're so beautiful," he said, tucking a few strands of hair behind my ear.

"You're not so bad yourself," I laughed, leaning forward to steal a kiss.

"You've been doing so much for me lately, as well as for my family," I said, my tone becoming serious. "I don't know how I'll ever begin to repay you."

Cam looked at me thoughtfully for a minute. "How about you love me for real?"

My heart skipped a beat.

"I mean it," he continued. "I know we started off with a fake marriage, a contract. But I have been in love with you for years."

I stared at him, wide-eyed. I searched his face for any sign that this was a joke, but I only saw seriousness. He was telling the truth. He really loved me. Tears began to prick at the back of my eyes.

"When you're not around, I worry about you. I wonder what you're doing. I miss you when you're gone. Whenever you're here, I want you to do everything within my power to make you smile, to keep you safe. I even get jealous when you so much as look at another man," he laughed. "If that's not love, I don't know what is."

'Cam, I . . ." I trailed off.

He shook his head. "I've always loved you. And according to my father, everyone knew about it too," he said, referring to the letter his father left me.

"This is all I've ever wanted too," I said softly, tears flowing down my face. Cam gently caught them with his thumb, wiping them away.

"So what do you say, Mrs. Luxmore?" he said, his eyes twinkling. "Would you want to make our relationship real? Will you be my wife? Be with me for the rest of our lives?"

I nodded and Cam leaned in for a kiss. "I love you," I whispered.

"I never knew how sexy the words 'I love you' could be," Cam murmured against my lips. "Hearing them from you is the sexiest thing I've ever heard." He tilted my head up so I was looking into his eyes. "Say it again," he whispered.

I smiled at my husband. "I love you," I said, meaning it more than I've ever meant anything in my entire life. "I love you so damn much."

Epilogue

One Year Later

WHAT A YEAR IT'S BEEN. A few days after Julia's house renovations, the reading of Walter's will had taken place.

Camden had successfully inherited everything that was once his father's - all of his businesses and contacts, his shares, even a few houses.

As expected, Desmond was left with nothing. He was understandably enraged and had fought, unsuccessfully, to regain any sort of power. He was promptly removed and banned from all Luxmore Inc properties. Every access, every privilege, even his wealth was restricted and removed.

After a lengthy investigation that had started years before his father's death, Desmond was arrested for fraud and embezzlement within the company, as well as a few different drug charges. Without his father or his influence, Desmond wouldn't be seeing the light of day anytime soon.

As a result of all this, Monica left him, ending their engagement. Without his power, and more importantly his money, she had no reason to stay. She never truly loved him, only his wealth and the privileges that came with his last name.

Julia and her family are absolutely thriving. Tyler has made a complete recovery and is as healthy as he possibly could be. He'll still have regular check-ups and everything, but other than that, he's just your average teenager.

As for me and Camden...

He surprised me by planning a real wedding for us. I had a custom-made dress that had me feeling like a princess. He even let me help out with a lot of the details this time around.

And more importantly, I had my sister by my side.

Her and Lisa were my two bridesmaids. Since Desmond was in prison, John and Terry were standing by Camden's side during the ceremony. He had more powerful friends he could have chosen instead, but these three were so important to me that Cam suggested they all stand up with us. I wouldn't have it any other way. I wouldn't have gotten through the past couple of years if it wasn't for the three of them.

They weren't just my coworkers, they were my best friends.

Julia's kids served as our ring bearers and flower girls, loving every minute of their roles.

Situated in the front row next to his mother, who was beaming proudly, was a memorial left for his father. We all wished he could have been here. He would have been so proud of the man that Camden has become.

Standing up in front of everyone we loved, we recited our new vows, pledging our love and devotion to one another.

I smiled as tears ran down my face. After everything that happened the past couple of years I never thought we'd make it here. And I've never been happier.

As we were pronounced husband and wife Cam tipped me backwards, kissing me as our guests clapped and cheered.

"You have no idea how much I love you, Mrs. Luxmore."

"Pretty sure I love you more," I teased with a wink.

We turned towards the guests, walking down the aisle officially as husband and wife.

I couldn't ask for a better life.